Conan: The Defining Stories

Robert E. Howard

Shadows in the Moonlight *(Robert E. Howard)*

1. A swift crashing of horses through the tall reeds; a heavy fall, a despairing cry. From the dying steed there staggered up its rider, a slender girl in sandals and girdled tunic. Her dark hair fell over her white shoulders, her eyes were those of a trapped animal. She did not look at the jungle of reeds that hemmed in the little clearing, nor at the blue waters that lapped the low shore behind her. Her wide-eyed gaze was fixed in agonized intensity on the horseman who pushed through the reedy screen and dismounted before her.

He was a tall man, slender, but hard as steel. From head to heel he was clad in light silvered mesh-mail that fitted his supple form like a glove. From under the dome-shaped, gold-chased helmet his brown eyes regarded her mockingly.

'Stand back!' her voice shrilled with terror. 'Touch me not, Shah Amurath, or I will throw myself into the water and drown!'

He laughed, and his laughter was like the purr of a sword sliding from a silken sheath.

'No, you will not drown, Olivia, daughter of confusion, for the marge is too shallow, and I can catch you before you can reach the deeps. You gave me a merry chase, by the gods, and all my men are far behind us. But there is no horse west of Vilayet that can distance Irem for long.' He nodded at the tall, slender-legged desert stallion behind him.

'Let me go!' begged the girl, tears of despair staining her face. 'Have I not suffered enough? Is there any humiliation, pain or degradation you have not heaped on me? How long must my torment last?'

'As long as I find pleasure in your whimperings, your pleas, tears and writhings,' he answered with a smile that would have seemed gentle to a stranger. 'You are strangely virile, Olivia. I wonder if I shall ever weary of you, as I have always wearied of women before. You are ever fresh and unsullied, in spite of me. Each new day with you brings a new delight.

'But come—let us return to Akif, where the people are still feting the conqueror of the miserable kozaki; while he, the conqueror, is engaged in recapturing a wretched fugitive, a foolish, lovely, idiotic runaway!'

'No!' She recoiled, turning toward the waters lapping bluely among the reeds.

'Yes!' His flash of open anger was like a spark struck from flint. With a quickness her tender limbs could not approximate, he caught her wrist, twisting it in pure wanton cruelty until she screamed and sank to her knees.

'Slut! I should drag you back to Akif at my horse's tail, but I will be merciful and carry you on my saddle-bow, for which favor you shall humbly thank me, while—'

He released her with a startled oath and sprang back, his saber flashing out, as a terrible apparition burst from the reedy jungle sounding an inarticulate cry of hate.

Olivia, staring up from the ground, saw what she took to be either a savage or a madman advancing on Shah Amurath in an attitude of deadly menace. He was powerfully built, naked but for a girdled loincloth, which was stained with blood and crusted with dried mire. His black mane was matted with mud and clotted blood; there were streaks of dried blood on his chest and limbs, dried blood on the long straight sword he gripped in his right hand. From under the tangle of his locks, bloodshot eyes glared like coals of blue fire.

'You Hyrkanian dog!' mouthed this apparition in a barbarous accent. 'The devils of vengeance have brought you here!'

'Kozak!' ejaculated Shah Amurath, recoiling. 'I did not know a dog of you escaped! I thought you all lay stiff on the steppe, by Ilbars River.'

'All but me, damn you!' cried the other. 'Oh, I've dreamed of such a meeting as this, while I crawled on my belly through the brambles, or lay under rocks while the ants gnawed my flesh, or crouched in the mire up to my mouth—I dreamed, but never hoped it would come to pass. Oh, gods of Hell, how I have yearned for this!'

The stranger's bloodthirsty joy was terrible to behold. His jaws champed spasmodically, froth appeared on his blackened lips.

'Keep back!' ordered Shah Amurath, watching him narrowly.

'Ha!' It was like the bark of a timber wolf. 'Shah Amurath, the great Lord of Akif! Oh, damn you, how I love the sight of you— you, who fed my comrades to the vultures, who tore them between wild horses, blinded and maimed and mutilated them— ai, you dog, you filthy dog!' His voice rose to a maddened scream, and he charged.

In spite of the terror of his wild appearance, Olivia looked to see him fall at the first crossing of the blades. Madman or savage, what could he do, naked, against the mailed chief of Akif?

There was an instant when the blades flamed and licked, seeming barely to touch each other and leap apart; then the broadsword flashed past the saber and descended terrifically on Shah Amurath's shoulder. Olivia cried out at the fury of that stroke. Above the crunch of the rending mail, she distinctly heard the snap of the shoulder-bone. The Hyrkanian reeled back, suddenly ashen, blood spurting over the links of his hauberk; his saber slipped from his nerveless fingers.

'Quarter!' he gasped.

'Quarter?' There was a quiver of frenzy in the stranger's voice. 'Quarter such as you gave us, you swine!'

Olivia closed her eyes. This was no longer battle, but butchery, frantic, bloody, impelled by an hysteria of fury and hate, in which culminated the sufferings of battle, massacre, torture, and fear-ridden, thirst-maddened, hunger-haunted flight. Though Olivia knew that Shah Amurath deserved no mercy or pity from any living creature, yet she closed her eyes and pressed her hands over her ears, to shut out the sight of that dripping sword that rose and fell with the sound of a butcher's cleaver, and the gurgling cries that dwindled away and ceased.

She opened her eyes, to see the stranger turning away from a gory travesty that only vaguely resembled a human being. The man's breast heaved with exhaustion or passion; his brow was beaded with sweat; his right hand was splashed with blood.

He did not speak to her, or even glance toward her. She saw him stride through the reeds that grew at the water's edge, stoop, and tug at something. A boat wallowed out of its hiding-place among the stalks. Then she divined his intention, and was galvanized into action.

'Oh, wait!' she wailed, staggering up and running toward him. 'Do not leave me! Take me with you!'

He wheeled and stared at her. There was a difference in his bearing. His bloodshot eyes were sane. It was as if the blood he had just shed had quenched the fire of his frenzy.

'Who are you?' he demanded.

'I am called Olivia. I was his captive. I ran away. He followed me. That's why he came here. Oh, do not leave me here! His warriors are not far behind him. They will find his corpse—they will find me near it—oh!' She moaned in her terror and wrung her white hands.

He stared at her in perplexity.

'Would you be better off with me?' he demanded. 'I am a barbarian, and I know from your looks that you fear me.'

'Yes, I fear you,' she replied, too distracted to dissemble. 'My flesh crawls at the horror of your aspect. But I fear the Hyrkanians more. Oh, let me go with you! They will put me to the torture if they find me beside their dead lord.'

'Come, then.' He drew aside, and she stepped quickly into the boat, shrinking from contact with him. She seated herself in the bow, and he stepped into the boat, pushed off with an oar, and using it as a paddle, worked his way tortuously among the tall stalks until they glided out into open water. Then he set to work with both oars, rowing with great, smooth, even strokes, the heavy muscles of arms and shoulders and back rippling in rhythm to his exertions.

There was silence for some time, the girl crouching in the bows, the man tugging at the oars. She watched him with timorous fascination. It was evident that he was not an Hyrkanian, and he did not resemble the Hyborian races. There was a wolfish hardness about him that marked the barbarian. His features, allowing for the strains and stains of battle and his hiding in the marshes, reflected that same untamed wildness, but they were neither evil nor degenerate.

'Who are you?' she asked. 'Shah Amurath called you a kozak; were you of that band?'

'I am Conan, of Cimmeria,' he grunted. 'I was with the kozaki, as the Hyrkanian dogs called us.'

She knew vaguely that the land he named lay far to the northwest, beyond the farthest boundaries of the different kingdoms of her race.

'I am a daughter of the King of Ophir,' she said. 'My father sold me to a Shemite chief, because I would not marry a prince of Koth.'

The Cimmerian grunted in surprize.

Her lips twisted in a bitter smile. 'Aye, civilized men sell their children as slaves to savages, sometimes. They call your race barbaric, Conan of Cimmeria.'

'We do not sell our children,' he growled, his chin jutting truculently.

'Well—I was sold. But the desert man did not misuse me. He wished to buy the good will of Shah Amurath, and I was among the gifts he brought to Akif of the purple gardens. Then—' She shuddered and hid her face in her hands.

'I should be lost to all shame,' she said presently. 'Yet each memory stings me like a slaver's whip. I abode in Shah Amurath's palace, until some weeks agone he rode out with his hosts to do battle with a band of invaders who were ravaging the borders of Turan. Yesterday he returned in triumph, and a great fete was made to honor him. In the drunkenness and rejoicing, I found an opportunity to steal out of the city on a stolen horse. I had thought to escape—but he followed, and about midday came up with me. I outran his vassals, but him I could not escape. Then you came.'

'I was lying hid in the reeds,' grunted the barbarian. 'I was one of those dissolute rogues, the Free Companions, who burned and looted along the borders. There were five thousand of us, from a score of races and tribes. We had been serving as mercenaries for a rebel prince in eastern Koth, most of us, and when he made peace with his cursed sovereign, we were out of employment; so we took to plundering the outlying dominions of Koth, Zamora and Turan impartially. A week ago Shah Amurath trapped us near the banks of Ilbars with fifteen thousand men. Mitra! The skies were black with vultures. When the lines broke, after a whole day of fighting, some tried to break through to the north, some to the west. I doubt if any escaped. The steppes were covered with horsemen riding down the fugitives. I broke for the east, and finally reached the edge of the marshes that border this part of Vilayet.

'I've been hiding in the morasses ever since. Only the day before yesterday the riders ceased beating up the reed-brakes, searching for just such fugitives as I. I've squirmed and burrowed and hidden like a snake, feasting on musk-rats I caught and ate raw, for lack of fire to cook them. This dawn I found this boat hidden among the reeds. I hadn't intended going out on the sea until night, but after I killed Shah Amurath, I knew his mailed dogs would be close at hand.'

'And what now?'

'We shall doubtless be pursued. If they fail to see the marks left by the boat, which I covered as well as I could, they'll guess anyway that we took to sea, after they fail to find us among the marshes. But we have a start, and I'm going to haul at these oars until we reach a safe place.'

'Where shall we find that?' she asked hopelessly. 'Vilayet is an Hyrkanian pond.'

'Some folk don't think so,' grinned Conan grimly; 'notably the slaves that have escaped from galleys and become pirates.'

'But what are your plans?'

'The southwestern shore is held by the Hyrkanians for hundreds of miles. We still have a long way to go before we pass beyond their northern boundaries. I intend to go northward until I think we have passed them. Then we'll turn westward, and try to land on the shore bordered by the uninhabited steppes.'

'Suppose we meet pirates, or a storm?' she asked. 'And we shall starve on the steppes.'

'Well,' he reminded her, 'I didn't ask you to come with me.'

'I am sorry.' She bowed her shapely dark head. 'Pirates, storms, starvation—they are all kinder than the people of Turan.'

'Aye.' His dark face grew somber. 'I haven't done with them yet. Be at ease, girl. Storms are rare on Vilayet at this time of year. If we make the steppes, we shall not starve. I was reared in a naked land. It was those cursed marshes, with their stench and stinging flies, that nigh unmanned me. I am at home in the high lands. As for pirates—' He grinned enigmatically, and bent to the oars.

The sun sank like a dull-glowing copper ball into a lake of fire. The blue of the sea merged with the blue of the sky, and both turned to soft dark velvet, clustered with stars and the mirrors of stars. Olivia reclined in the bows of the gently rocking boat, in a state dreamy and unreal. She experienced an illusion that she was floating in midair, stars beneath her as well as above. Her silent companion was etched vaguely against the softer darkness. There was no break or falter in the rhythm of his oars; he might have been a fantasmal oarsman, rowing her across the dark lake of Death. But the edge of her fear was dulled, and, lulled by the monotony of motion, she passed into a quiet slumber.

Dawn was in her eyes when she awakened, aware of a ravenous hunger. It was a change in the motion of the boat that had roused her; Conan was resting on his oars, gazing beyond her. She realized that he had rowed all night without pause, and marvelled at his iron endurance. She twisted about to follow his stare, and saw a green wall of trees and shrubbery rising from the water's edge and sweeping away in a wide curve, enclosing a small bay whose waters lay still as blue glass.

'This is one of the many islands that dot this inland sea,' said Conan. 'They are supposed to be uninhabited. I've heard the Hyrkanians seldom visit them. Besides, they generally hug the shores in their galleys, and we have come a long way. Before sunset we were out of sight of the mainland.'

With a few strokes he brought the boat in to shore and made the painter fast to the arching root of a tree which rose from the water's edge. Stepping ashore, he reached out a hand to help Olivia. She took it, wincing slightly at the bloodstains upon it, feeling a hint of the dynamic strength that lurked in the barbarian's thews.

A dreamy quiet lay over the woods that bordered the blue bay. Then somewhere, far back among the trees, a bird lifted its morning song. A breeze whispered through the leaves, and set them to murmuring. Olivia found herself listening intently for something, she knew not what. What might be lurking amid those nameless woodlands?

As she peered timidly into the shadows between the trees, something swept into the sunlight with a swift whirl of wings: a great parrot which dropped on to a leafy branch and swayed there, a gleaming image of jade and crimson. It turned its crested head sidewise and regarded the invaders with glittering eyes of jet.

'Crom!' muttered the Cimmerian. 'Here is the grandfather of all parrots. He must be a thousand years old! Look at the evil wisdom of his eyes. What mysteries do you guard, Wise Devil?'

Abruptly the bird spread its flaming wings and, soaring from its perch, cried out harshly: 'Yagkoolan yok tha, xuthalla!' and with a wild screech of horribly human laughter, rushed away through the trees to vanish in the opalescent shadows.

Olivia stared after it, feeling the cold hand of nameless foreboding touch her supple spine.

'What did it say?' she whispered.

'Human words, I'll swear,' answered Conan; 'but in what tongue I can't say.'

'Nor I,' returned the girl. 'Yet it must have learned them from human lips. Human, or—' she gazed into the leafy fastness and shuddered slightly, without knowing why.

'Crom, I'm hungry!' grunted the Cimmerian. 'I could eat a whole buffalo. We'll look for fruit; but first I'm going to cleanse myself of this dried mud and blood. Hiding in marshes is foul business.'

So saying, he laid aside his sword, and wading out shoulder-deep into the blue water, went about his ablutions. When he emerged, his clean-cut bronze limbs shone, his streaming black mane was no longer matted. His blue eyes, though they smoldered with unquenchable fire, were no longer murky or bloodshot. But the tigerish suppleness of limb and the dangerous aspect of feature were not altered.

Strapping on his sword once more, he motioned the girl to follow him, and they left the shore, passing under the leafy arches of the great branches. Underfoot lay a short green sward which cushioned their tread. Between the trunks of the trees they caught glimpses of faery-like vistas.

Presently Conan grunted in pleasure at the sight of golden and russet globes hanging in clusters among the leaves. Indicating that the girl should seat herself on a fallen tree, he filled her lap with the exotic delicacies, and then himself fell to with unconcealed gusto.

'Ishtar!' said he, between mouthfuls. 'Since Ilbars I have lived on rats, and roots I dug out of the stinking mud. This is sweet to the palate, though not very filling. Still, it will serve if we eat enough.'

Olivia was too busy to reply. The sharp edge of the Cimmerian's hunger blunted, he began to gaze at his fair companion with more interest than previously, noting the lustrous clusters of her dark hair, the peach-bloom tints of her dainty skin, and the rounded contours of her lithe figure which the scanty silk tunic displayed to full advantage.

Finishing her meal, the object of his scrutiny looked up, and meeting his burning, slit-eyed gaze, she changed color and the remnants of the fruit slipped from her fingers.

Without comment, he indicated with a gesture that they should continue their explorations, and rising, she followed him out of the trees and into a glade, the farther end of which was bounded by a dense thicket. As they stepped into the open there was a ripping crash in this thicket, and Conan, bounding aside and carrying the girl with him, narrowly saved them from something that rushed through the air and struck a tree-trunk with a thunderous impact.

Whipping out his sword, Conan bounded across the glade and plunged into the thicket. Silence ensued, while Olivia crouched on the sward, terrified and bewildered. Presently Conan emerged, a puzzled scowl on his face.

'Nothing in that thicket,' he growled. 'But there was something—'

He studied the missile that had so narrowly missed them, and grunted incredulously, as if unable to credit his own senses. It was a huge block of greenish stone which lay on the sward at the foot of the tree, whose wood its impact had splintered.

'A strange stone to find on an uninhabited island,' growled Conan.

Olivia's lovely eyes dilated in wonder. The stone was a symmetrical block, indisputably cut and shaped by human hands. And it was astonishingly massive. The Cimmerian grasped it with both hands, and with legs braced and the muscles standing out on his arms and back in straining knots, he heaved it above his head and cast it from him, exerting every ounce of nerve and sinew. It fell a few feet in front of him. Conan swore.

'No man living could throw that rock across this glade. It's a task for siege engines. Yet here there are no mangonels or ballistas.'

'Perhaps it was thrown by some such engine from afar,' she suggested.

He shook his head. 'It didn't fall from above. It came from yonder thicket. See how the twigs are broken? It was thrown as a man might throw a pebble. But who? What? Come!'

She hesitantly followed him into the thicket. Inside the outer ring of leafy brush, the undergrowth was less dense. Utter silence brooded over all. The springy sward gave no sign of footprint. Yet from this mysterious thicket had hurtled that boulder, swift and deadly. Conan bent closer to the sward, where the grass was crushed down here and there. He shook his head angrily. Even to his keen eyes it gave no clue as to what had stood or trodden there. His gaze roved to the green roof above their heads, a solid ceiling of thick leaves and interwoven arches. And he froze suddenly.

Then rising, sword in hand, he began to back away, thrusting Olivia behind him.

'Out of here, quick!' he urged in a whisper that congealed the girl's blood.

'What is it? What do you see?'

'Nothing,' he answered guardedly, not halting his wary retreat.

'But what is it, then? What lurks in this thicket?'

'Death!' he answered, his gaze still fixed on the brooding jade arches that shut out the sky.

Once out of the thicket, he took her hand and led her swiftly through the thinning trees, until they mounted a grassy slope, sparsely treed, and emerged upon a low plateau, where the grass grew taller and the trees were few and scattered. And in the midst of that plateau rose a long broad structure of crumbling greenish stone.

They gazed in wonder. No legends named such a building on any island of Vilayet. They approached it warily, seeing that moss and lichen crawled over the stones, and the broken roof gaped to the sky. On all sides lay bits and shards of masonry, half hidden in the waving grass, giving the impression that once many buildings rose there, perhaps a whole town. But now only the long hall-like structure rose against the sky, and its walls leaned drunkenly among the crawling vines.

Whatever doors had once guarded its portals had long rotted away. Conan and his companion stood in the broad entrance and stared inside. Sunlight streamed in through gaps in the walls and roof, making the interior a dim weave of light and shadow. Grasping his sword firmly, Conan entered, with the slouching gait of a hunting panther, sunken head and noiseless feet. Olivia tiptoed after him.

Once within, Conan grunted in surprise, and Olivia stifled a scream.

'Look! Oh, look!'

'I see,' he answered. 'Nothing to fear. They are statues.'

'But how life-like—and how evil!' she whispered, drawing close to him.

They stood in a great hall, whose floor was of polished stone, littered with dust and broken stones, which had fallen from the ceiling. Vines, growing between the stones, masked the apertures. The lofty roof, flat and undomed, was upheld by thick columns, marching in rows down the sides of the walls. And in each space between these columns stood a strange figure.

They were statues, apparently of iron, black and shining as if continually polished. They were life-sized, depicting tall, lithely powerful men, with cruel hawk-like faces. They were naked, and every swell, depression and contour of joint and sinew was represented with incredible realism. But the most life-like feature was their proud, intolerant faces. These features were not cast in the same mold. Each face possessed its own individual characteristics, though there was a tribal likeness between them all. There was none of the monotonous uniformity of decorative art, in the faces at least.

'They seem to be listening—and waiting!' whispered the girl uneasily.

Conan rang his hilt against one of the images.

'Iron,' he pronounced. 'But Crom! In what molds were they cast?'

He shook his head and shrugged his massive shoulders in puzzlement.

Olivia glanced timidly about the great silent hall. Only the ivy-grown stones, the tendril-clasped pillars, with the dark figures brooding between them, met her gaze. She shifted uneasily and wished to be gone, but the images held a strange fascination for her companion. He examined them in detail, and barbarian-like, tried to break off their limbs. But their material resisted his best efforts. He could neither disfigure nor dislodge from its niche a single image. At last he desisted, swearing in his wonder.

'What manner of men were these copied from?' he inquired of the world at large. 'These figures are black, yet they are not like negroes. I have never seen their like.'

'Let us go into the sunlight,' urged Olivia, and he nodded, with a baffled glance at the brooding shapes along the walls.

So they passed out of the dusky hall into the clear blaze of the summer sun. She was surprized to note its position in the sky; they had spent more time in the ruins than she had guessed.

'Let us take to the boat again,' she suggested. 'I am afraid here. It is a strange evil place. We do not know when we may be attacked by whatever cast the rock.'

'I think we're safe as long as we're not under the trees,' he answered. 'Come.'

The plateau, whose sides fell away toward the wooded shores on the east, west and south, sloped upward toward the north to abut on a tangle of rocky cliffs, the highest point of the island. Thither Conan took his way, suiting his long stride to his companion's gait. From time to time his glance rested inscrutably upon her, and she was aware of it.

They reached the northern extremity of the plateau, and stood gazing up the steep pitch of the cliffs. Trees grew thickly along the rim of the plateau east and west of the cliffs, and clung to the precipitous incline. Conan glanced at these trees suspiciously, but he began the ascent, helping his companion on the climb. The slope was not sheer, and was broken by ledges and boulders. The Cimmerian, born in a hill country, could have run up it like a cat, but Olivia found the going difficult. Again and again she felt herself lifted lightly off her feet and over some obstacle that would have taxed her strength to surmount, and her wonder grew at the sheer physical power of the man. She no longer found his touch repugnant. There was a promise of protection in his iron clasp.

At last they stood on the ultimate pinnacle, their hair stirring in the sea wind. From their feet the cliffs fell away sheerly three or four hundred feet to a narrow tangle of woodlands bordering the beach. Looking southward they saw the whole island lying like a great oval mirror, its bevelled edges sloping down swiftly into a rim of green, except where it broke in the pitch of the cliffs. As far as they could see, on all sides stretched the blue waters, still, placid, fading into dreamy hazes of distance.

'The sea is still,' sighed Olivia. 'Why should we not take up our journey again?'

Conan, poised like a bronze statue on the cliffs, pointed northward. Straining her eyes, Olivia saw a white fleck that seemed to hang suspended in the aching haze.

'What is it?'

'A sail.'

'Hyrkanians?'

'Who can tell, at this distance?'

'They will anchor here—search the island for us!' she cried in quick panic.

'I doubt it. They come from the north, so they can not be searching for us. They may stop for some other reason, in which case we'll have to hide as best we can. But I believe it's either pirate, or an Hyrkanian galley returning from some northern raid. In the latter case they are not likely to anchor here. But we can't put to sea until they've gone out of sight, for they're coming from the direction in which we must go. Doubtless they'll pass the island tonight, and at dawn we can go on our way.'

'Then we must spend the night here?' she shivered.

'It's safest.'

'Then let us sleep here, on the crags,' she urged.

He shook his head, glancing at the stunted trees, at the marching woods below, a green mass which seemed to send out tendrils straggling up the sides of the cliffs.

'Here are too many trees. We'll sleep in the ruins.'

She cried out in protest.

'Nothing will harm you there,' he soothed. 'Whatever threw the stone at us did not follow us out of the woods. There was nothing to show that any wild thing lairs in the ruins. Besides, you are soft-skinned, and used to shelter and dainties. I could sleep naked in the snow and feel no discomfort, but the dew would give you cramps, were we to sleep in the open.'

Olivia helplessly acquiesced, and they descended the cliffs, crossed the plateau and once more approached the gloomy, age-haunted ruins. By this time the sun was sinking below the plateau rim. They had found fruit in the trees near the cliffs, and these formed their supper, both food and drink.

The southern night swept down quickly, littering the dark blue sky with great white stars, and Conan entered the shadowy ruins, drawing the reluctant Olivia after him. She shivered at the sight of those tense black shadows in their niches along the walls. In the darkness that the starlight only faintly touched, she could not make out their outlines; she could only sense their attitude of waiting—waiting as they had waited for untold centuries.

Conan had brought a great armful of tender branches, well leafed. These he heaped to make a couch for her, and she lay upon it, with a curious sensation as of one lying down to sleep in a serpent's lair.

Whatever her forebodings, Conan did not share them. The Cimmerian sat down near her, his back against a pillar, his sword across his knees. His eyes gleamed like a panther's in the dusk.

'Sleep, girl,' said he. 'My slumber is light as a wolf's. Nothing can enter this hall without awaking me.'

Olivia did not reply. From her bed of leaves she watched the immobile figure, indistinct in the soft darkness. How strange, to move in fellowship with a barbarian, to be cared for and protected by one of a race, tales of which had frightened her as a child! He came of a people bloody, grim and ferocious. His kinship to the wild was apparent in his every action; it burned in his smoldering eyes. Yet he had not harmed her, and her worst oppressor had been a man the world called civilized. As a delicious languor stole over her relaxing limbs and she sank into foamy billows of slumber, her last waking thought was a drowsy recollection of the firm touch of Conan's fingers on her soft flesh.

2. Olivia dreamed, and through her dreams crawled a suggestion of lurking evil, like a black serpent writhing through flower gardens. Her dreams were fragmentary and colorful, exotic shards of a broken, unknown pattern, until they crystalized into a scene of horror and madness, etched against a background of cyclopean stones and pillars.

She saw a great hall, whose lofty ceiling was upheld by stone columns marching in even rows along the massive walls. Among these pillars fluttered great green and scarlet parrots, and the hall was thronged with black-skinned, hawk-faced warriors. They were not negroes. Neither they nor their garments nor weapons resembled anything of the world the dreamer knew.

They were pressing about one bound to a pillar: a slender white-skinned youth, with a cluster of golden curls about his alabaster brow. His beauty was not altogether human—like the dream of a god, chiseled out of living marble.

The black warriors laughed at him, jeered and taunted in a strange tongue. The lithe naked form writhed beneath their cruel hands. Blood trickled down the ivory thighs to spatter on the polished floor. The screams of the victim echoed through the hall; then lifting his head toward the ceiling and the skies beyond, he cried out a name in an awful voice. A dagger in an ebon hand cut short his cry, and the golden head rolled on the ivory breast.

As if in answer to that desperate cry, there was a rolling thunder as of celestial chariot-wheels, and a figure stood before the slayers, as if materialized out of empty air. The form was of a man, but no mortal man ever wore such an aspect of inhuman beauty. There was an unmistakable resemblance between him and the youth who dropped lifeless in his chains, but the alloy of humanity that softened the godliness of the youth was lacking in the features of the stranger, awful and immobile in their beauty.

The blacks shrank back before him, their eyes slits of fire. Lifting a hand, he spoke, and his tones echoed through the silent halls in deep rich waves of sound. Like men in a trance the black warriors fell back until they were ranged along the walls in regular lines. Then from the stranger's chiseled lips rang a terrible invocation and command: 'Yagkoolan yok tha, xuthalla!'

At the blast of that awful cry, the black figures stiffened and froze. Over their limbs crept a curious rigidity, an unnatural petrification. The stranger touched the limp body of the youth, and the chains fell away from it. He lifted the corpse in his arms;

then ere he turned away, his tranquil gaze swept again over the silent rows of ebony figures, and he pointed to the moon, which gleamed in through the casements. And they understood, those tense, waiting statues that had been men....

Olivia awoke, starting up on her couch of branches, a cold sweat beading her skin. Her heart pounded loud in the silence. She glanced wildly about. Conan slept against his pillar, his head fallen upon his massive breast. The silvery radiance of the late moon crept through the gaping roof, throwing long white lines along the dusty floor. She could see the images dimly, black, tense—waiting. Fighting down a rising hysteria, she saw the moonbeams rest lightly on the pillars and the shapes between.

What was that? A tremor among the shadows where the moonlight fell. A paralysis of horror gripped her, for where there should have been the immobility of death, there was movement: a slow twitching, a flexing and writhing of ebon limbs—an awful scream burst from her lips as she broke the bonds that held her mute and motionless. At her shriek Conan shot erect, teeth gleaming, sword lifted.

'The statues! The statues!—Oh my God, the statues are coming to life!'

And with the cry she sprang through a crevice in the wall, burst madly through the hindering vines, and ran, ran, ran—blind, screaming, witless—until a grasp on her arm brought her up short and she shrieked and fought against the arms that caught her, until a familiar voice penetrated the mists of her terror, and she saw Conan's face, a mask of bewilderment in the moonlight.

'What in Crom's name, girl? Did you have a nightmare?' His voice sounded strange and far away. With a sobbing gasp she threw her arms about his thick neck and clung to him convulsively, crying in panting catches.

'Where are they? Did they follow us?'

'Nobody followed us,' he answered.

She sat up, still clinging to him, and looked fearfully about. Her blind flight had carried her to the southern edge of the plateau. Just below them was the slope, its foot masked in the thick shadows of the woods. Behind them she saw the ruins looming in the high-swinging moon.

'Did you not see them?—The statues, moving, lifting their hands, their eyes glaring in the shadows?'

'I saw nothing,' answered the barbarian uneasily. 'I slept more soundly than usual, because it has been so long since I have slumbered the night through; yet I don't think anything could have entered the hall without waking me.'

'Nothing entered,' a laugh of hysteria escaped her. 'It was something there already. Ah, Mitra, we lay down to sleep among them, like sheep making their bed in the shambles!'

'What are you talking about?' he demanded. 'I woke at your cry, but before I had time to look about me, I saw you rush out through the crack in the wall. I pursued you, lest you come to harm. I thought you had a nightmare.'

'So I did!' she shivered. 'But the reality was more grisly than the dream. Listen!' And she narrated all that she had dreamed and thought to see.

Conan listened attentively. The natural skepticism of the sophisticated man was not his. His mythology contained ghouls, goblins, and necromancers. After she had finished, he sat silent, absently toying with his sword.

'The youth they tortured was like the tall man who came?' he asked at last.

'As like as son to father,' she answered, and hesitantly: 'If the mind could conceive of the offspring of a union of divinity with humanity, it would picture that youth. The gods of old times mated sometimes with mortal women, our legends tell us.'

'What gods?' he muttered.

'The nameless, forgotten ones. Who knows? They have gone back into the still waters of the lakes, the quiet hearts of the hills, the gulfs beyond the stars. Gods are no more stable than men.'

'But if these shapes were men, blasted into iron images by some god or devil, how can they come to life?'

'There is witchcraft in the moon,' she shuddered. 'He pointed at the moon; while the moon shines on them, they live. So I believe.'

'But we were not pursued,' muttered Conan, glancing toward the brooding ruins. 'You might have dreamed they moved. I am of a mind to return and see.'

'No, no!' she cried, clutching him desperately. 'Perhaps the spell upon them holds them in the hall. Do not go back! They will rend you limb from limb! Oh, Conan, let us go into our boat and flee this awful island! Surely the Hyrkanian ship has passed us now! Let us go!'

So frantic was her pleading that Conan was impressed. His curiosity in regard to the images was balanced by his superstition. Foes of flesh and blood he did not fear, however great the odds, but any hint of the supernatural roused all the dim monstrous instincts of fear that are the heritage of the barbarian.

He took the girl's hand and they went down the slope and plunged into the dense woods, where the leaves whispered, and nameless night-birds murmured drowsily. Under the trees the shadows clustered thick, and Conan swerved to avoid the denser patches. His eyes roved continuously from side to side, and often flitted into the branches above them. He went quickly yet warily, his arm girdling the girl's waist so strongly that she felt as if she were being carried rather than guided. Neither spoke. The only sound was the girl's quick nervous panting, the rustle of her small feet in the grass. So they came through the trees to the edge of the water, shimmering like molten silver in the moonlight.

'We should have brought fruit for food,' muttered Conan; 'but doubtless we'll find other islands. As well leave now as later; it's but a few hours till dawn—'

His voice trailed away. The painter was still made fast to the looping root. But at the other end was only a smashed and shattered ruin, half submerged in the shallow water.

A stifled cry escaped Olivia. Conan wheeled and faced the dense shadows, a crouching image of menace. The noise of the night-birds was suddenly silent. A brooding stillness reigned over the woods. No breeze moved the branches, yet somewhere the leaves stirred faintly.

Quick as a great cat Conan caught up Olivia and ran. Through the shadows he raced like a phantom, while somewhere above and behind them sounded a curious rushing among the leaves, that implacably drew closer and closer. Then the moonlight burst full upon their faces, and they were speeding up the slope of the plateau.

At the crest Conan laid Olivia down, and turned to glare back at the gulf of shadows they had just quitted. The leaves shook in a sudden breeze; that was all. He shook his mane with an angry growl. Olivia crept to his feet like a frightened child. Her eyes looked up at him, dark wells of horror.

'What are we to do, Conan?' she whispered.

He looked at the ruins, stared again into the woods below.

'We'll go to the cliffs,' he declared, lifting her to her feet. 'Tomorrow I'll make a raft, and we'll trust our luck to the sea again.'

'It was not—not they that destroyed our boat?' It was half question, half assertion.

He shook his head, grimly taciturn.

Every step of the way across that moon-haunted plateau was a sweating terror for Olivia, but no black shapes stole subtly from

the looming ruins, and at last they reached the foot of the crags, which rose stark and gloomily majestic above them. There Conan halted in some uncertainty, at last selecting a place sheltered by a broad ledge, nowhere near any trees.

'Lie down and sleep if you can, Olivia,' he said. 'I'll keep watch.'

But no sleep came to Olivia, and she lay watching the distant ruins and the wooded rim until the stars paled, the east whitened, and dawn in rose and gold struck fire from the dew on the grass-blades.

She rose stiffly, her mind reverting to all the happenings of the night. In the morning light some of its terrors seemed like figments of an overwrought imagination. Conan strode over to her, and his words electrified her.

'Just before dawn I heard the creak of timbers and the rasp and clack of cordage and oars. A ship has put in and anchored at the beach not far away—probably the ship whose sail we saw yesterday. We'll go up the cliffs and spy on her.'

Up they went, and lying on their bellies among the boulders, saw a painted mast jutting up beyond the trees to the west.

'An Hyrkanian craft, from the cut of her rigging,' muttered Conan. 'I wonder if the crew—'

A distant medley of voices reached their ears, and creeping to the southern edge of the cliffs, they saw a motley horde emerge from the fringe of trees along the western rim of the plateau, and stand there a space in debate. There was much flourishing of arms, brandishing of swords, and loud rough argument. Then the whole band started across the plateau toward the ruins, at a slant that would take them close by the foot of the cliffs.

'Pirates!' whispered Conan, a grim smile on his thin lips. 'It's an Hyrkanian galley they've captured. Here—crawl among these rocks.

'Don't show yourself unless I call to you,' he instructed, having secreted her to his satisfaction among a tangle of boulders along the crest of the cliffs. 'I'm going to meet these dogs. If I succeed in my plan, all will be well, and we'll sail away with them. If I don't succeed—well, hide yourself in the rocks until they're gone, for no devils on this island are as cruel as these sea-wolves.'

And tearing himself from her reluctant grasp, he swung quickly down the cliffs.

Looking fearfully from her eyrie, Olivia saw the band had neared the foot of the cliffs. Even as she looked, Conan stepped out from among the boulders and faced them, sword in hand. They gave back with yells of menace and surprise; then halted uncertainly to glare at this figure which had appeared so suddenly from the rocks. There were some seventy of them, a wild horde made up of men from many nations: Kothians, Zamorians, Brythunians, Corinthians, Shemites. Their features reflected the wildness of their natures. Many bore the scars of the lash or the branding-iron. There were cropped ears, slit noses, gaping eye-sockets, stumps of wrists—marks of the hangman as well as scars of battle. Most of them were half naked, but the garments they wore were fine; gold-braided jackets, satin girdles, silken breeches, tattered, stained with tar and blood, vied with pieces of silver-chased armor. Jewels glittered in nose-rings and ear-rings, and in the hilts of their daggers.

Over against this bizarre mob stood the tall Cimmerian in strong contrast with his hard bronzed limbs and clean-cut vital features.

'Who are you?' they roared.

'Conan the Cimmerian!' His voice was like the deep challenge of a lion. 'One of the Free Companions. I mean to try my luck with the Red Brotherhood. Who's your chief?'

'I, by Ishtar!' bellowed a bull-like voice, as a huge figure swaggered forward: a giant, naked to the waist, where his capacious belly was girdled by a wide sash that upheld voluminous silken pantaloons. His head was shaven except for a scalp-lock, his mustaches dropped over a rat-trap mouth. Green Shemitish slippers with upturned toes were on his feet, a long straight sword in his hand.

Conan stared and glared.

'Sergius of Khrosha, by Crom!'

'Aye, by Ishtar!' boomed the giant, his small black eyes glittering with hate. 'Did you think I had forgot? Ha! Sergius never forgets an enemy. Now I'll hang you up by the heels and skin you alive. At him, lads!'

'Aye, send your dogs at me, big-belly,' sneered Conan with bitter scorn. 'You were always a coward, you Kothic cur.'

'Coward! To me?' The broad face turned black with passion. 'On guard, you northern dog! I'll cut out your heart!'

In an instant the pirates had formed a circle about the rivals, their eyes blazing, their breath sucking between their teeth in bloodthirsty enjoyment. High up among the crags Olivia watched, sinking her nails into her palms in her painful excitement.

Without formality the combatants engaged, Sergius coming in with a rush, quick on his feet as a giant cat, for all his bulk. Curses hissed between his clenched teeth as he lustily swung and parried. Conan fought in silence, his eyes slits of blue bale-fire.

The Kothian ceased his oaths to save his breath. The only sounds were the quick scuff of feet on the sward, the panting of the pirate, the ring and clash of steel. The swords flashed like white fire in the early sun, wheeling and circling. They seemed to recoil from each other's contact, then leap together again instantly. Sergius was giving back; only his superlative skill had saved him thus far from the blinding speed of the Cimmerian's onslaught. A louder clash of steel, a sliding rasp, a choking cry—from the pirate horde a fierce yell split the morning as Conan's sword plunged through their captain's massive body. The point quivered an instant from between Sergius's shoulders, a hand's breadth of white fire in the sunlight; then the Cimmerian wrenched back his steel and the pirate chief fell heavily, face down, and lay in a widening pool of blood, his broad hands twitching for an instant.

Conan wheeled toward the gaping corsairs.

'Well, you dogs!' he roared. 'I've sent your chief to hell. What says the law of the Red Brotherhood?'

Before any could answer, a rat-faced Brythunian, standing behind his fellows, whirled a sling swiftly and deadly. Straight as an arrow sped the stone to its mark, and Conan reeled and fell as a tall tree falls to the woodsman's ax. Up on the cliff Olivia caught at the boulders for support. The scene swam dizzily before her eyes; all she could see was the Cimmerian lying limply on the sward, blood oozing from his head.

The rat-faced one yelped in triumph and ran to stab the prostrate man, but a lean Corinthian thrust him back.

'What, Aratus, would you break the law of the Brotherhood, you dog?'

'No law is broken,' snarled the Brythunian.

'No law? Why, you dog, this man you have just struck down is by just rights our captain!'

'Nay!' shouted Aratus. 'He was not of our band, but an outsider. He had not been admitted to fellowship. Slaying Sergius does not make him captain, as would have been the case had one of us killed him.'

'But he wished to join us,' retorted the Corinthian. 'He said so.'

At that a great clamor arose, some siding with Aratus, some with the Corinthian, whom they called Ivanos. Oaths flew thick, challenges were passed, hands fumbled at sword-hilts.

At last a Shemite spoke up above the clamor: 'Why do you argue over a dead man?'

'He's not dead,' answered the Corinthian, rising from beside the prostrate Cimmerian. 'It was a glancing blow; he's only stunned.'

At that the clamor rose anew, Aratus trying to get at the senseless man and Ivanos finally bestriding him, sword in hand, and defying all and sundry. Olivia sensed that it was not so much in defense of Conan that the Corinthian took his stand, but in opposition to Aratus. Evidently these men had been Sergius's lieutenants, and there was no love lost between them. After more arguments, it was decided to bind Conan and take him along with them, his fate to be voted on later.

The Cimmerian, who was beginning to regain consciousness, was bound with leather girdles, and then four pirates lifted him, and with many complaints and curses, carried him along with the band, which took up its journey across the plateau once more. The body of Sergius was left where it had fallen; a sprawling, unlovely shape on the sun-washed sward.

Up among the rocks, Olivia lay stunned by the disaster. She was incapable of speech or action, and could only lie there and stare with horrified eyes as the brutal horde dragged her protector away.

How long she lay there, she did not know. Across the plateau she saw the pirates reach the ruins and enter, dragging their captive. She saw them swarming in and out of the doors and crevices, prodding into the heaps of debris, and clambering about the walls. After awhile a score of them came back across the plateau and vanished among the trees on the western rim, dragging the body of Sergius after them, presumably to cast into the sea. About the ruins the others were cutting down trees and securing material for a fire. Olivia heard their shouts, unintelligible in the distance, and she heard the voices of those who had gone into the woods, echoing among the trees. Presently they came back into sight, bearing casks of liquor and leathern sacks of food. They headed for the ruins, cursing lustily under their burdens.

Of all this Olivia was but mechanically cognizant. Her overwrought brain was almost ready to collapse. Left alone and unprotected, she realized how much the protection of the Cimmerian had meant to her. There intruded vaguely a wonderment at the mad pranks of Fate, that could make the daughter of a king the companion of a red-handed barbarian. With it came a revulsion toward her own kind. Her father, and Shah Amurath, they were civilized men. And from them she had had only suffering. She had never encountered any civilized man who treated her with kindness unless there was an ulterior motive behind his actions. Conan had shielded her, protected her, and—so far—demanded nothing in return. Laying her head in her rounded arms she wept, until distant shouts of ribald revelry roused her to her own danger.

She glanced from the dark ruins about which the fantastic figures, small in the distance, weaved and staggered, to the dusky depths of the green forest. Even if her terrors in the ruins the night before had been only dreams, the menace that lurked in those green leafy depths below was no figment of nightmare. Were Conan slain or carried away captive, her only choice would lie between giving herself up to the human wolves of the sea, or remaining alone on that devil-haunted island.

As the full horror of her situation swept over her, she fell forward in a swoon.

3. The sun was hanging low when Olivia regained her senses. A faint wind wafted to her ears distant shouts and snatches of ribald song. Rising cautiously, she looked out across the plateau. She saw the pirates clustered about a great fire outside the ruins, and her heart leaped as a group emerged from the interior dragging some object she knew was Conan. They propped him against the wall, still evidently bound fast, and there ensued a long discussion, with much brandishing of weapons. At last they dragged him back into the hall, and took up anew the business of ale-guzzling. Olivia sighed; at least she knew that the

Cimmerian still lived. Fresh determination steeled her. As soon as night fell, she would steal to those grim ruins and free him or be taken herself in the attempt. And she knew it was not selfish interest alone which prompted her decision.

With this in mind she ventured to creep from her refuge to pluck and eat nuts which grew sparsely near at hand. She had not eaten since the day before. It was while so occupied that she was troubled by a sensation of being watched. She scanned the rocks nervously, then, with a shuddering suspicion, crept to the north edge of the cliff and gazed down into the waving green mass below, already dusky with the sunset. She saw nothing; it was impossible that she could be seen, when not on the cliff's edge, by anything lurking in those woods. Yet she distinctly felt the glare of hidden eyes, and felt that something animate and sentient was aware of her presence and her hiding-place.

Stealing back to her rocky eyrie, she lay watching the distant ruins until the dusk of night masked them, and she marked their position by the flickering flames about which black figures leaped and cavorted groggily.

Then she rose. It was time to make her attempt. But first she stole back to the northern edge of the cliffs, and looked down into the woods that bordered the beach. And as she strained her eyes in the dim starlight, she stiffened, and an icy hand touched her heart.

Far below her something moved. It was as if a black shadow detached itself from the gulf of shadows below her. It moved slowly up the sheer face of the cliff—a vague bulk, shapeless in the semi-darkness. Panic caught Olivia by the throat, and she struggled with the scream that tugged at her lips. Turning, she fled down the southern slope.

That flight down the shadowed cliffs was a nightmare in which she slid and scrambled, catching at jagged rocks with cold fingers. As she tore her tender skin and bruised her soft limbs on the rugged boulders over which Conan had so lightly lifted her, she realized again her dependence on the iron-thewed barbarian.

But this thought was but one in a fluttering maelstrom of dizzy fright.

The descent seemed endless, but at last her feet struck the grassy levels, and in a very frenzy of eagerness she sped away toward the fire that burned like the red heart of night. Behind her, as she fled, she heard a shower of stones rattle down the steep slope, and the sound lent wings to her heels. What grisly climber dislodged those stones she dared not try to think.

Strenuous physical action dissipated her blind terror somewhat and before she had reached the ruin, her mind was clear, her reasoning faculties alert, though her limbs trembled from her efforts.

She dropped to the sward and wriggled along on her belly until, from behind a small tree that had escaped the axes of the pirates, she watched her enemies. They had completed their supper, but were still drinking, dipping pewter mugs or jewelled goblets into the broken heads of the wine-casks. Some were already snoring drunkenly on the grass, while others had staggered into the ruins. Of Conan she saw nothing. She lay there, while the dew formed on the grass about her and the leaves overhead, and the men about the fire cursed, gambled and argued. There were only a few about the fire; most of them had gone into the ruins to sleep.

She lay watching them, her nerves taut with the strain of waiting, the flesh crawling between her shoulders at the thought of what might be watching her in turn—of what might be stealing up behind her. Time dragged on leaden feet. One by one the revellers sank down in drunken slumber, until all were stretched senseless beside the dying fire.

Olivia hesitated—then was galvanized by a distant glow rising through the trees. The moon was rising!

With a gasp she rose and hurried toward the ruins. Her flesh crawled as she tiptoed among the drunken shapes that sprawled beside the gaping portal. Inside were many more; they shifted and mumbled in their besotted dreams, but none awakened as she glided among them. A sob of joy rose to her lips as she saw Conan. The Cimmerian was wide awake, bound upright to a pillar, his eyes gleaming in the faint reflection of the waning fire outside.

Picking her way among the sleepers, she approached him. Lightly as she had come, he had heard her; had seen her when first framed in the portal. A faint grin touched his hard lips.

She reached him and clung to him an instant. He felt the quick beating of her heart against his breast. Through a broad crevice in the wall stole a beam of moonlight, and the air was instantly supercharged with subtle tension. Conan felt it and stiffened. Olivia felt it and gasped. The sleepers snored on. Bending quickly, she drew a dagger from its senseless owner's belt, and set to work on Conan's bonds. They were sail cords, thick and heavy, and tied with the craft of a sailor. She toiled desperately, while the tide of moonlight crept slowly across the floor toward the feet of the crouching black figures between the pillars.

Her breath came in gasps; Conan's wrists were free, but his elbows and legs were still bound fast. She glanced fleetingly at the figures along the walls—waiting, waiting. They seemed to watch her with the awful patience of the undead. The drunkards beneath her feet began to stir and groan in their sleep. The moonlight crept down the hall, touching the black feet. The cords fell from Conan's arms, and taking the dagger from her, he ripped the bonds from his legs with a single quick slash. He stepped out from the pillar, flexing his limbs, stoically enduring the agony of returning circulation. Olivia crouched against him, shaking like a leaf. Was it some trick of the moonlight that touched the eyes of the black figures with fire, so that they glimmered redly in the shadows?

Conan moved with the abruptness of a jungle cat. Catching up his sword from where it lay in a stack of weapons near by, he lifted Olivia lightly from her feet and glided through an opening that gaped in the ivy-grown wall.

No word passed between them. Lifting her in his arms he set off swiftly across the moon-bathed sward. Her arms about his iron neck, the Ophirean closed her eyes, cradling her dark curly head against his massive shoulder. A delicious sense of security stole over her.

In spite of his burden, the Cimmerian crossed the plateau swiftly, and Olivia, opening her eyes, saw that they were passing under the shadow of the cliffs.

'Something climbed the cliffs,' she whispered. 'I heard it scrambling behind me as I came down.'

'We'll have to chance it,' he grunted.

'I am not afraid—now,' she sighed.

'You were not afraid when you came to free me, either,' he answered. 'Crom, what a day it has been! Such haggling and wrangling I never heard. I'm nearly deaf. Aratus wished to cut out my heart, and Ivanos refused, to spite Aratus, whom he hates. All day long they snarled and spat at one another, and the crew quickly grew too drunk to vote either way—'

He halted suddenly, an image of bronze in the moonlight. With a quick gesture he tossed the girl lightly to one side and behind him. Rising to her knees on the soft sward, she screamed at what she saw.

Out of the shadows of the cliffs moved a monstrous shambling bulk—an anthropomorphic horror, a grotesque travesty of creation.

In general outline it was not unlike a man. But its face, limned in the bright moonlight, was bestial, with close-set ears, flaring nostrils, and a great flabby-lipped mouth in which gleamed white tusk-like fangs. It was covered with shaggy grayish hair, shot with silver which shone in the moonlight, and its great misshapen paws hung nearly to the earth. Its bulk was tremendous; as it stood on its short bowed legs, its bullet-head rose above that of the man who faced it; the sweep of the hairy breast and giant shoulders was breathtaking; the huge arms were like knotted trees.

The moonlight scene swam, to Olivia's sight. This, then, was the end of the trail—for what human being could withstand the fury of that hairy mountain of thews and ferocity? Yet as she stared in wide-eyed horror at the bronzed figure facing the monster, she sensed a kinship in the antagonists that was almost appalling. This was less a struggle between man and beast than a conflict between two creatures of the wild, equally merciless and ferocious. With a flash of white tusks, the monster charged.

The mighty arms spread wide as the beast plunged, stupefyingly quick for all his vast bulk and stunted legs.

Conan's action was a blur of speed Olivia's eye could not follow. She only saw that he evaded that deadly grasp, and his sword, flashing like a jet of white lightning, sheared through one of those massive arms between shoulder and elbow. A great spout of blood deluged the sward as the severed member fell, twitching horribly, but even as the sword bit through, the other malformed hand locked in Conan's black mane.

Only the iron neck-muscles of the Cimmerian saved him from a broken neck that instant. His left hand darted out to clamp on the beast's squat throat, his left knee was jammed hard against the brute's hairy belly. Then began a terrific struggle, which lasted only seconds, but which seemed like ages to the paralyzed girl.

The ape maintained his grasp in Conan's hair, dragging him toward the tusks that glistened in the moonlight. The Cimmerian resisted this effort, with his left arm rigid as iron, while the sword in his right hand, wielded like a butcher-knife, sank again and again into the groin, breast and belly of his captor. The beast took its punishment in awful silence, apparently unweakened by the blood that gushed from its ghastly wounds. Swiftly the terrible strength of the anthropoid overcame the leverage of braced arm and knee. Inexorably Conan's arm bent under the strain; nearer and nearer he was drawn to the slavering jaws that gaped for his life. Now the blazing eyes of the barbarian glared into the bloodshot eyes of the ape. But as Conan tugged vainly at his sword, wedged deep in the hairy body, the frothing jaws snapped spasmodically shut, an inch from the Cimmerian's face, and he was hurled to the sward by the dying convulsions of the monster.

Olivia, half fainting, saw the ape heaving, thrashing and writhing, gripping, man-like, the hilt that jutted from its body. A sickening instant of this, then the great bulk quivered and lay still.

Conan rose and limped over to the corpse. The Cimmerian breathed heavily, and walked like a man whose joints and muscles have been wrenched and twisted almost to their limit of endurance. He felt his bloody scalp and swore at the sight of the long black red-stained strands still grasped in the monster's shaggy hand.

'Crom!' he panted. 'I feel as if I'd been racked! I'd rather fight a dozen men. Another instant and he'd have bitten off my head. Blast him, he's torn a handful of my hair out by the roots.'

Gripping his hilt with both hands he tugged and worked it free. Olivia stole close to clasp his arm and stare down wide-eyed at the sprawling monster.

'What—what is it?' she whispered.

'A gray man-ape,' he grunted. 'Dumb, and man-eating. They dwell in the hills that border the eastern shore of this sea. How this one got to this island, I can't say. Maybe he floated here on driftwood, blown out from the mainland in a storm.'

'And it was he that threw the stone?'

'Yes; I suspected what it was when we stood in the thicket and I saw the boughs bending over our heads. These creatures always lurk in the deepest woods they can find, and seldom emerge. What brought him into the open, I can't say, but it was lucky for us; I'd have had no chance with him among the trees.'

'It followed me,' she shivered. 'I saw it climbing the cliffs.'

'And following his instinct, he lurked in the shadow of the cliff, instead of following you out across the plateau. His kind are creatures of darkness and the silent places, haters of sun and moon.'

'Do you suppose there are others?'

'No, else the pirates had been attacked when they went through the woods. The gray ape is wary, for all his strength, as shown by his hesitancy in falling upon us in the thicket. His lust for you must have been great, to have driven him to attack us finally in the open. What—'

He started and wheeled back toward the way they had come. The night had been split by an awful scream. It came from the ruins.

Instantly there followed a mad medley of yells, shrieks and cries of blasphemous agony. Though accompanied by a ringing of steel, the sounds were of massacre rather than battle.

Conan stood frozen, the girl clinging to him in a frenzy of terror. The clamor rose to a crescendo of madness, and then the Cimmerian turned and went swiftly toward the rim of the plateau, with its fringe of moon-limned trees. Olivia's legs were trembling so that she could not walk; so he carried her, and her heart calmed its frantic pounding as she nestled into his cradling arms.

They passed under the shadowy forest, but the clusters of blackness held no terrors, the rifts of silver discovered no grisly shape. Night-birds murmured slumberously. The yells of slaughter dwindled behind them, masked in the distance to a confused jumble of sound. Somewhere a parrot called, like an eery echo: 'Yagkoolan yok tha, xuthalla!' So they came to the tree-fringed water's edge and saw the galley lying at anchor, her sail shining white in the moonlight. Already the stars were paling for dawn.

4. In the ghastly whiteness of dawn a handful of tattered, blood-stained figures staggered through the trees and out on to the narrow beach. There were forty-four of them, and they were a cowed and demoralized band. With panting haste they plunged into the water and began to wade toward the galley, when a stern challenge brought them up standing.

Etched against the whitening sky they saw Conan the Cimmerian standing in the bows, sword in hand, his black mane tossing in the dawn wind.

'Stand!' he ordered. 'Come no nearer. What would you have, dogs?'

'Let us come aboard!' croaked a hairy rogue fingering a bloody stump of ear. 'We'd be gone from this devil's island.'

'The first man who tries to climb over the side, I'll split his skull,' promised Conan.

They were forty-four to one, but he held the whip-hand. The fight had been hammered out of them.

'Let us come aboard, good Conan,' whined a red-sashed Zamorian, glancing fearfully over his shoulder at the silent woods. 'We have been so mauled, bitten, scratched and rended, and are so weary from fighting and running, that not one of us can lift a sword.'

'Where is that dog Aratus?' demanded Conan.

'Dead, with the others! It was devils fell upon us! They were rending us to pieces before we could awake—a dozen good rovers died in their sleep. The ruins were full of flame-eyed shadows, with tearing fangs and sharp talons.'

'Aye!' put in another corsair. 'They were the demons of the isle, which took the forms of molten images, to befool us. Ishtar! We lay down to sleep among them. We are no cowards. We fought them as long as mortal man may strive against the powers of darkness. Then we broke away and left them tearing at the corpses like jackals. But surely they'll pursue us.'

'Aye, let us come aboard!' clamored a lean Shemite. 'Let us come in peace, or we must come sword in hand, and though we be so weary you will doubtless slay many of us, yet you can not prevail against us many.'

'Then I'll knock a hole in the planks and sink her,' answered Conan grimly. A frantic chorus of expostulation rose, which Conan silenced with a lion-like roar.

'Dogs! Must I aid my enemies? Shall I let you come aboard and cut out my heart?'

'Nay, nay!' they cried eagerly. 'Friends—friends, Conan. We are thy comrades! We be all lusty rogues together. We hate the king of Turan, not each other.'

Their gaze hung on his brown, frowning face.

'Then if I am one of the Brotherhood,' he grunted, 'the laws of the Trade apply to me; and since I killed your chief in fair fight, then I am your captain!'

There was no dissent. The pirates were too cowed and battered to have any thought except a desire to get away from that island of fear. Conan's gaze sought out the blood-stained figure of the Corinthian.

'How, Ivanos!' he challenged. 'You took my part, once. Will you uphold my claims again?'

'Aye, by Mitra!' The pirate, sensing the trend of feeling, was eager to ingratiate himself with the Cimmerian. 'He is right, lads; he is our lawful captain!'

A medley of acquiescence rose, lacking enthusiasm perhaps, but with sincerity accentuated by the feel of the silent woods behind them which might mask creeping ebony devils with red eyes and dripping talons.

'Swear by the hilt,' Conan demanded.

Forty-four sword-hilts were lifted toward him, and forty-four voices blended in the corsair's oath of allegiance.

Conan grinned and sheathed his sword. 'Come aboard, my bold swashbucklers, and take the oars.'

He turned and lifted Olivia to her feet, from where she had crouched shielded by the gunwales.

'And what of me, sir?' she asked.

'What would you?' he countered, watching her narrowly.

'To go with you, wherever your path may lie!' she cried, throwing her white arms about his bronzed neck.

The pirates, clambering over the rail, gasped in amazement.

'To sail a road of blood and slaughter?' he questioned. 'This keel will stain the blue waves crimson wherever it plows.'

'Aye, to sail with you on blue seas or red,' she answered passionately. 'You are a barbarian, and I am an outcast, denied by my people. We are both pariahs, wanderers of earth. Oh, take me with you!'

With a gusty laugh he lifted her to his fierce lips.

'I'll make you Queen of the Blue Sea! Cast off there, dogs! We'll scorch King Yildiz's pantaloons yet, by Crom!'

Shadows in Zamboula (*Robert E. Howard*)

1 A Drum Begins

'Peril hides in the house of Aram Baksh!'

The speaker's voice quivered with earnestness and his lean, black-nailed fingers clawed at Conan's mightily muscled arm as he croaked his warning. He was a wiry, sun-burnt man with a straggling black beard, and his ragged garments proclaimed him a nomad. He looked smaller and meaner than ever in contrast to the giant Cimmerian with his black brows, broad chest, and powerful limbs. They stood in a corner of the Sword-Makers' Bazar, and on either side of them flowed past the many-tongued, many-colored stream of the Zamboula streets, which is exotic, hybrid, flamboyant and clamorous.

Conan pulled his eyes back from following a bold-eyed, red-lipped Ghanara whose short skirt bared her brown thigh at each insolent step, and frowned down at his importunate companion.

'What do you mean by peril?' he demanded.

The desert man glanced furtively over his shoulder before replying, and lowered his voice.

'Who can say? But desert men and travelers have slept in the house of Aram Baksh, and never been seen or heard of again. What became of them? He swore they rose and went their way— and it is true that no citizen of the city has ever disappeared from his house. But no one saw the travelers again, and men say that goods and equipment recognized as theirs have been seen in the bazars. If Aram did not sell them, after doing away with their owners, how came they here?'

'I have no goods,' growled the Cimmerian, touching the shagreen-bound hilt of the broadsword that hung at his hip. 'I have even sold my horse.'

'But it is not always rich strangers who vanish by night from the house of Aram Baksh!' chattered the Zuagir. 'Nay, poor desert men have slept there—because his score is less than that of the other taverns—and have been seen no more. Once a chief of the Zuagirs whose son had thus vanished complained to the satrap, Jungir Khan, who ordered the house searched by soldiers.'

'And they found a cellar full of corpses?' asked Conan in good-humored derision.

'Nay! They found naught! And drove the chief from the city with threats and curses! But—' he drew closer to Conan and shivered—'something else was found! At the edge of the desert, beyond the houses, there is a clump of palm trees, and within that grove there is a pit. And within that pit have been found human bones, charred and blackened! Not once, but many times!'

'Which proves what?' grunted the Cimmerian.

'Aram Baksh is a demon! Nay, in this accursed city which Stygians built and which Hyrkanians rule—where white, brown and black folk mingle together to produce hybrids of all unholy hues and breeds—who can tell who is a man, and who a demon in disguise? Aram Baksh is a demon in the form of a man! At night he assumes his true guise and carries his guests off into the desert where his fellow demons from the waste meet in conclave.'

'Why does he always carry off strangers?' asked Conan skeptically.

'The people of the city would not suffer him to slay their people, but they care naught for the strangers who fall into his hands. Conan, you are of the West, and know not the secrets of this ancient land. But, since the beginning of happenings, the demons of the desert have worshipped Yog, the Lord of the Empty Abodes, with fire—fire that devours human victims.

'Be warned! You have dwelt for many moons in the tents of the Zuagirs, and you are our brother! Go not to the house of Aram Baksh!'

'Get out of sight!' Conan said suddenly. 'Yonder comes a squad of the city-watch. If they see you they may remember a horse that was stolen from the satrap's stable'

The Zuagir gasped, and moved convulsively. He ducked between a booth and a stone horse-trough, pausing only long enough to

chatter: 'Be warned, my brother! There are demons in the house of Aram Baksh!' Then he darted down a narrow alley and was gone.

Conan shifted his broad sword-belt to his liking, and calmly returned the searching stares directed at him by the squad of watchmen as they swung past. They eyed him curiously and suspiciously, for he was a man who stood out even in such a motley throng as crowded the winding streets of Zamboula. His blue eyes and alien features distinguished him from the Eastern swarms, and the straight sword at his hip added point to the racial difference.

The watchmen did not accost him, but swung on down the street, while the crowd opened a lane for them. They were Pelishtim, squat, hook-nosed, with blue-black beards sweeping their mailed breasts—mercenaries hired for work the ruling Turanians considered beneath themselves, and no less hated by the mongrel population for that reason.

Conan glanced at the sun, just beginning to dip behind the flat-topped houses on the western side of the bazar, and hitching once more at his belt, moved off in the direction of Aram Baksh's tavern.

With a hillman's stride he moved through the ever-shifting colors of the streets, where the ragged tunics of whining beggars brushed against the ermine-trimmed khalats of lordly merchants, and the pearl-sewn satin of rich courtezans. Giant black slaves slouched along, jostling blue-bearded wanderers from the Shemitish cities, ragged nomads from the surrounding deserts, traders and adventurers from all the lands of the East.

The native population was no less heterogenous. Here, centuries ago, the armies of Stygia had come, carving an empire out of the eastern desert. Zamboula was but a small trading-town then, lying amidst a ring of oases, and inhabited by descendants of nomads. The Stygians built it into a city and settled it with their own people, and with Shemite and Kushite slaves. The ceaseless caravans, threading the desert from east to west and back again, brought riches and more mingling of races. Then came the conquering Turanians, riding out of the East to thrust back the boundaries of Stygia, and now for a generation Zamboula had been Turan's westernmost outpost, ruled by a Turanian satrap.

The babel of a myriad tongues smote on the Cimmerian's ears as the restless pattern of the Zamboula streets weaved about him— cleft now and then by a squad of clattering horsemen, the tall, supple warriors of Turan, with dark hawk-faces, clinking metal and curved swords. The throng scampered from under their horses' hoofs, for they were the lords of Zamboula. But tall, somber Stygians, standing back in the shadows, glowered darkly, remembering their ancient glories. The hybrid population cared little whether the king who controlled their destinies dwelt in dark Khemi or gleaming Aghrapur. Jungir Khan ruled Zamboula, and men whispered that Nafertari, the satrap's mistress, ruled Jungir Khan; but the people went their way, flaunting their myriad colors in the streets, bargaining, disputing, gambling, swilling, loving, as the people of Zamboula have done for all the centuries its towers and minarets have lifted over the sands of the Kharamun.

Bronze lanterns, carved with leering dragons, had been lighted in the streets before Conan reached the house of Aram Baksh. The tavern was the last occupied house on the street, which ran west. A wide garden, enclosed by a wall, where date-palms grew thick, separated it from the houses farther east. To the west of the inn stood another grove of palms, through which the street, now become a road, wound out into the desert. Across the road from the tavern stood a row of deserted huts, shaded by straggling palm trees, and occupied only by bats and jackals. As Conan came down the road he wondered why the beggars, so plentiful in Zamboula, had not appropriated these empty houses for sleeping quarters. The lights ceased some distance behind him. Here were no lanterns, except the one hanging before the tavern gate: only the stars, the soft dust of the road underfoot, and the rustle of the palm leaves in the desert breeze.

Aram's gate did not open upon the road, but upon the alley which ran between the tavern and the garden of the date-palms. Conan jerked lustily at the rope which depended from the bell beside the lantern, augmenting its clamor by hammering on the iron-bound teakwork gate with the hilt of his sword. A wicket opened in the gate and a black face peered through.

'Open, blast you,' requested Conan. 'I'm a guest. I've paid Aram for a room, and a room I'll have, by Crom!'

The black craned his neck to stare into the starlit road behind Conan; but he opened the gate without comment, and closed it again behind the Cimmerian, locking and bolting it. The wall was unusually high; but there were many thieves in Zamboula, and a house on the edge of the desert might have to be defended against a nocturnal nomad raid. Conan strode through a garden where great pale blossoms nodded in the starlight, and entered the tap-room, where a Stygian with the shaven head of a student sat at a table brooding over nameless mysteries, and some nondescripts wrangled over a game of dice in a corner.

Aram Baksh came forward, walking softly, a portly man, with a black beard that swept his breast, a jutting hook-nose, and small black eyes which were never still.

'You wish food?' he asked. 'Drink?'

'I ate a joint of beef and a loaf of bread in the suk,' grunted Conan. 'Bring me a tankard of Ghazan wine—I've got just enough left to pay for it.' He tossed a copper coin on the wine-splashed board.

'You did not win at the gaming-tables?'

'How could I, with only a handful of silver to begin with? I paid you for the room this morning, because I knew I'd probably lose. I wanted to be sure I had a roof over my head tonight. I notice nobody sleeps in the streets in Zamboula. The very beggars hunt a niche they can barricade before dark. The city must be full of a particularly blood-thirsty brand of thieves.'

He gulped the cheap wine with relish, and then followed Aram out of the tap-room. Behind him the players halted their game to stare after him with a cryptic speculation in their eyes. They said nothing, but the Stygian laughed, a ghastly laugh of inhuman cynicism and mockery. The others lowered their eyes uneasily, avoiding one another's glance. The arts studied by a Stygian scholar are not calculated to make him share the feelings of a normal human being.

Conan followed Aram down a corridor lighted by copper lamps, and it did not please him to note his host's noiseless tread. Aram's feet were clad in soft slippers and the hallway was carpeted with thick Turanian rugs; but there was an unpleasant suggestion of stealthiness about the Zamboulan.

At the end of the winding corridor Aram halted at a door, across which a heavy iron bar rested in powerful metal brackets. This Aram lifted and showed the Cimmerian into a well-appointed chamber, the windows of which, Conan instantly noted, were small and strongly set with twisted bars of iron, tastefully gilded. There were rugs on the floor, a couch, after the Eastern fashion, and ornately carved stools. It was a much more elaborate chamber than Conan could have procured for the price nearer the center of the city—a fact that had first attracted him, when, that morning, he discovered how slim a purse his roisterings for the past few days had left him. He had ridden into Zamboula from the desert a week before.

Aram had lighted a bronze lamp, and he now called Conan's attention to the two doors. Both were provided with heavy bolts.

'You may sleep safely tonight, Cimmerian,' said Aram, blinking over his bushy beard from the inner doorway.

Conan grunted and tossed his naked broadsword on the couch.

'Your bolts and bars are strong; but I always sleep with steel by my side.'

Aram made no reply; he stood fingering his thick beard for a moment as he stared at the grim weapon. Then silently he withdrew, closing the door behind him. Conan shot the bolt into place, crossed the room, opened the opposite door and looked out. The room was on the side of the house that faced the road running west from the city. The door opened into a small court that was enclosed by a wall of its own. The end-walls, which shut it off from the rest of the tavern compound, were high and without entrances; but the wall that flanked the road was low, and there was no lock on the gate.

Conan stood for a moment in the door, the glow of the bronze lamp behind him, looking down the road to where it vanished among the dense palms. Their leaves rustled together in the faint breeze; beyond them lay the naked desert. Far up the street, in the other direction, lights gleamed and the noises of the city came faintly to him. Here was only starlight, the whispering of the palm leaves, and beyond that low wall, the dust of the road and the deserted huts thrusting their flat roofs against the low stars. Somewhere beyond the palm groves a drum began.

The garbled warnings of the Zuagir returned to him, seeming somehow less fantastic than they had seemed in the crowded, sunlit streets. He wondered again at the riddle of those empty huts. Why did the beggars shun them? He turned back into the chamber, shut the door and bolted it.

The light began to flicker, and he investigated, swearing when he found the palm oil in the lamp was almost exhausted. He started to shout for Aram, then shrugged his shoulders and blew out the light. In the soft darkness he stretched himself fully clad on the couch, his sinewy hand by instinct searching for and closing on the hilt of his broadsword. Glancing idly at the stars framed in the barred windows, with the murmur of the breeze through the palms in his ears, he sank into slumber with a vague consciousness of the muttering drum, out on the desert—the low rumble and mutter of a leather-covered drum, beaten with soft, rhythmic strokes of an open black hand....

2 The Night Skulkers

It was the stealthy opening of a door which awakened the Cimmerian. He did not awake as civilized men do, drowsy and drugged and stupid. He awoke instantly, with a clear mind, recognizing the sound that had interrupted his sleep. Lying there tensely in the dark he saw the outer door slowly open. In a widening crack of starlit sky he saw framed a great black bulk, broad, stooping shoulders and a misshapen head blocked out against the stars.

Conan felt the skin crawl between his shoulders. He had bolted that door securely. How could it be opening now, save by supernatural agency? And how could a human being possess a head like that outlined against the stars? All the tales he had heard in the Zuagir tents of devils and goblins came back to bead his flesh with clammy sweat. Now the monster slid noiselessly into the room, with a crouching posture and a shambling gait; and a familiar scent assailed the Cimmerian's nostrils, but did not reassure him, since Zuagir legendry represented demons as smelling like that.

Noiselessly Conan coiled his long legs under him; his naked sword was in his right hand, and when he struck it was as suddenly and murderously as a tiger lunging out of the dark. Not even a demon could have avoided that catapulting charge. His sword met and clove through flesh and bone, and something went heavily to the floor with a strangling cry. Conan crouched in the dark above it, sword dripping in his hand. Devil or beast or man, the thing was dead there on the floor. He sensed death as any wild thing senses it. He glared through the half-open door into the starlit court beyond. The gate stood open, but the court was empty.

Conan shut the door but did not bolt it. Groping in the darkness he found the lamp and lighted it. There was enough oil in it to burn for a minute or so. An instant later he was bending over the figure that sprawled on the floor in a pool of blood.

It was a gigantic black man, naked but for a loin-cloth. One hand still grasped a knotty-headed bludgeon. The fellow's kinky wool was built up into horn-like spindles with twigs and dried mud. This barbaric coiffure had given the head its misshapen appearance in the starlight. Provided with a clue to the riddle, Conan pushed back the thick red lips, and grunted as he stared down at teeth filed to points.

He understood now the mystery of the strangers who had disappeared from the house of Aram Baksh; the riddle of the black drum thrumming out there beyond the palm groves, and of that pit of charred bones—that pit where strange meat might be roasted under the stars, while black beasts squatted about to glut a hideous hunger. The man on the floor was a cannibal slave from Darfar.

There were many of his kind in the city. Cannibalism was not tolerated openly in Zamboula. But Conan knew now why people locked themselves in so securely at night, and why even beggars shunned the open alleys and doorless ruins. He grunted in disgust as he visualized brutish black shadows skulking up and down the nighted streets, seeking human prey—and such men as Aram Baksh to open the doors to them. The innkeeper was not a demon; he was worse. The slaves from Darfar were notorious thieves; there was no doubt that some of their pilfered loot found its way into the hands of Aram Baksh. And in return he sold them human flesh.

Conan blew out the light, stepped to the door and opened it, and ran his hand over the ornaments on the outer side. One of them was movable and worked the bolt inside. The room was a trap to catch human prey like rabbits. But this time instead of a rabbit it had caught a saber-toothed tiger.

Conan returned to the other door, lifted the bolt and pressed against it. It was immovable and he remembered the bolt on the other side. Aram was taking no chances either with his victims or the men with whom he dealt. Buckling on his sword-belt, the Cimmerian strode out into the court, closing the door behind him. He had no intention of delaying the settlement of his reckoning with Aram Baksh. He wondered how many poor devils had been bludgeoned in their sleep and dragged out of that room and down the road that ran through the shadowed palm groves to the roasting-pit.

He halted in the court. The drum was still muttering, and he caught the reflection of a leaping red glare through the groves. Cannibalism was more than a perverted appetite with the black men of Darfar; it was an integral element of their ghastly cult. The black vultures were already in conclave. But whatever flesh filled their bellies that night, it would not be his.

To reach Aram Baksh he must climb one of the walls which separated the small enclosure from the main compound. They were high, meant to keep out the man-eaters; but Conan was no swamp-bred black man; his thews had been steeled in boyhood on the sheer cliffs of his native hills. He was standing at the foot of the nearer wall when a cry echoed under the trees.

In an instant Conan was crouching at the gate, glaring down the road. The sound had come from the shadows of the huts across the road. He heard a frantic choking and gurgling such as might result from a desperate attempt to shriek, with a black hand fastened over the victim's mouth. A close-knit clump of figures emerged from the shadows beyond the huts, and started down the road—three huge black men carrying a slender, struggling figure between them. Conan caught the glimmer of pale limbs writhing in the starlight, even as, with a convulsive wrench, the captive slipped from the grasp of the brutal fingers and came flying up the road, a supple young woman, naked as the day she was born. Conan saw her plainly before she ran out of the road and into the shadows between the huts. The blacks were at her heels, and back in the shadows the figures merged and an intolerable scream of anguish and horror rang out.

Stirred to red rage by the ghoulishness of the episode, Conan raced across the road.

Neither victim nor abductors were aware of his presence until the soft swish of the dust about his feet brought them about, and then he was almost upon them, coming with the gusty fury of a hill wind. Two of the blacks turned to meet him, lifting their bludgeons. But they failed to estimate properly the speed at which he was coming. One of them was down, disemboweled, before he could strike, and wheeling cat-like, Conan evaded the stroke of the other's cudgel and lashed in a whistling counter-cut. The black's head flew into the air; the headless body took three staggering steps, spurting blood and clawing horribly at the air with groping hands, and then slumped to the dust.

The remaining cannibal gave back with a strangled yell, hurling his captive from him. She tripped and rolled in the dust, and the black fled in blind panic toward the city. Conan was at his heels. Fear winged the black feet, but before they reached the easternmost hut, he sensed death at his back, and bellowed like an ox in the slaughter-yards.

'Black dog of hell!' Conan drove his sword between the dusky shoulders with such vengeful fury that the broad blade stood out half its length from the black breast. With a choking cry the black stumbled headlong, and Conan braced his feet and dragged out his sword as his victim fell.

Only the breeze disturbed the leaves. Conan shook his head as a lion shakes its mane and growled his unsatiated blood-lust. But no more shapes slunk from the shadows, and before the huts the starlit road stretched empty. He whirled at the quick patter of feet behind him, but it was only the girl, rushing to throw herself on him and clasp his neck in a desperate grasp, frantic from terror of the abominable fate she had just escaped.

'Easy, girl,' he grunted. 'You're all right. How did they catch you?'

She sobbed something unintelligible. He forgot all about Aram Baksh as he scrutinized her by the light of the stars. She was white, though a very definite brunette, obviously one of Zamboula's many mixed breeds. She was tall, with a slender, supple form, as he was in a good position to observe. Admiration burned in his fierce eyes as he looked down on her splendid bosom and her lithe limbs, which still quivered from fright and exertion. He passed an arm around her flexible waist and said, reassuringly: 'Stop shaking, wench; you're safe enough.'

His touch seemed to restore her shaken sanity. She tossed back her thick, glossy locks and cast a fearful glance over her shoulder, while she pressed closer to the Cimmerian as if seeking security in the contact.

'They caught me in the streets,' she muttered, shuddering. 'Lying in wait, beneath a dark arch—black men, like great, hulking apes! Set have mercy on me! I shall dream of it!'

'What were you doing out on the streets this time of night?' he inquired, fascinated by the satiny feel of her sleek skin under his questing fingers.

She raked back her hair and stared blankly up into his face. She did not seem aware of his caresses.

'My lover,' she said. 'My lover drove me into the streets. He went mad and tried to kill me. As I fled from him I was seized by those beasts.'

'Beauty like yours might drive a man mad,' quoth Conan, running his fingers experimentally through her glossy tresses.

She shook her head, like one emerging from a daze. She no longer trembled, and her voice was steady.

'It was the spite of a priest—of Totrasmek, the high priest of Hanuman, who desires me for himself—the dog!'

'No need to curse him for that,' grinned Conan. 'The old hyena has better taste than I thought.'

She ignored the bluff compliment. She was regaining her poise swiftly.

'My lover is a—a young Turanian soldier. To spite me, Totrasmek gave him a drug that drove him mad. Tonight he snatched up a sword and came at me to slay me in his madness, but I fled from him into the streets. The negroes seized me and brought me to this—what was that?'

Conan had already moved. Soundlessly as a shadow he drew her behind the nearest hut, beneath the straggling palms. They stood in tense stillness, while the low mutterings both had heard grew louder until voices were distinguishable. A group of negroes, some nine or ten, were coming along the road from the direction of the city. The girl clutched Conan's arm and he felt the terrified quivering of her supple body against his.

Now they could understand the gutturals of the black men.

'Our brothers have already assembled at the pit,' said one. 'We have had no luck. I hope they have enough for us.'

'Aram promised us a man,' muttered another, and Conan mentally promised Aram something.

'Aram keeps his word,' grunted yet another. 'Many a man we have taken from his tavern. But we pay him well. I myself have given him ten bales of silk I stole from my master. It was good silk, by Set!'

The blacks shuffled past, bare splay feet scuffing up the dust, and their voices dwindled down the road.

'Well for us those corpses are lying behind these huts,' muttered Conan. 'If they look in Aram's death-room they'll find another. Let's begone.'

'Yes, let us hasten!' begged the girl, almost hysterical again. 'My lover is wandering somewhere in the streets alone. The negroes may take him.'

'A devil of a custom this is!' growled Conan, as he led the way toward the city, paralleling the road but keeping behind the huts and straggling trees. 'Why don't the citizens clean out these black dogs?'

'They are valuable slaves,' murmured the girl. 'There are so many of them they might revolt if they were denied the flesh for which they lust. The people of Zamboula know they skulk the streets at night, and all are careful to remain within locked doors, except when something unforeseen happens, as it did to me. The blacks prey on anything they catch, but they seldom catch anybody but strangers. The people of Zamboula are not concerned with the strangers that pass through the city.

'Such men as Aram Baksh sell these strangers to the blacks. He would not dare attempt such a thing with a citizen.'

Conan spat in disgust, and a moment later led his companion out into the road which was becoming a street, with still, unlighted houses on each side. Slinking in the shadows was not congenial to his nature.

'Where do you want to go?' he asked. The girl did not seem to object to his arm about her waist.

'To my house, to rouse my servants,' she answered. 'To bid them search for my lover. I do not wish the city—the priests—anyone—to know of his madness. He—he is a young officer with a promising future. Perhaps we can drive this madness from him if we can find him.'

'If we find him?' rumbled Conan. 'What makes you think I want to spend the night scouring the streets for a lunatic?'

She cast a quick glance into his face, and properly interpreted the gleam in his blue eyes. Any woman could have known that he would follow her wherever she led—for a while, at least. But being a woman, she concealed her knowledge of that fact.

'Please,' she began with a hint of tears in her voice, 'I have no one else to ask for help—you have been kind—'

'All right!' he grunted. 'All right! What's the young reprobate's name?'

'Why—Alafdhal. I am Zabibi, a dancing-girl. I have danced often before the satrap, Jungir Khan, and his mistress Nafertari, and before all the lords and royal ladies of Zamboula. Totrasmek desired me, and because I repulsed him, he made me the innocent tool of his vengeance against Alafdhal. I asked a love potion of Totrasmek, not suspecting the depth of his guile and hate. He gave me a drug to mix with my lover's wine, and he swore that when Alafdhal drank it, he would love me even more madly than ever, and grant my every wish. I mixed the drug secretly with my lover's wine. But having drunk, my lover went raving mad and things came about as I have told you. Curse Totrasmek, the hybrid snake—ahhh!'

She caught his arm convulsively and both stopped short. They had come into a district of shops and stalls, all deserted and unlighted, for the hour was late. They were passing an alley, and in its mouth a man was standing, motionless and silent. His head was lowered, but Conan caught the weird gleam of eery eyes regarding them unblinkingly. His skin crawled, not with fear of the sword in the man's hand, but because of the uncanny suggestion of his posture and silence. They suggested madness. Conan pushed the girl aside and drew his sword.

'Don't kill him!' she begged. 'In the name of Set, do not slay him! You are strong—overpower him!'

'We'll see,' he muttered, grasping his sword in his right hand and clenching his left into a mallet-like fist.

He took a wary step toward the alley—and with a horrible moaning laugh the Turanian charged. As he came he swung his sword, rising on his toes as he put all the power of his body behind the blows. Sparks flashed blue as Conan parried the blade, and the next instant the madman was stretched senseless in the dust from a thundering buffet of Conan's left fist.

The girl ran forward.

'Oh, he is not—he is not—'

Conan bent swiftly, turned the man on his side and ran quick fingers over him.

'He's not hurt much,' he grunted. 'Bleeding at the nose, but anybody's likely to do that, after a clout on the jaw. He'll come to after a bit, and maybe his mind will be right. In the meantime I'll tie his wrists with his sword-belt—so. Now where do you want me to take him?'

'Wait!' She knelt beside the senseless figure, seized the bound hands and scanned them avidly. Then, shaking her head as if in baffled disappointment, she rose. She came close to the giant Cimmerian, and laid her slender hands on his arching breast. Her dark eyes, like wet black jewels in the starlight, gazed up into his.

'You are a man! Help me! Totrasmek must die! Slay him for me!'

'And put my neck into a Turanian noose?' he grunted.

'Nay!' The slender arms, strong as pliant steel, were around his corded neck. Her supple body throbbed against his. 'The Hyrkanians have no love for Totrasmek. The priests of Set fear him. He is a mongrel, who rules men by fear and superstition. I worship Set, and the Turanians bow to Erlik, but Totrasmek sacrifices to Hanuman the accursed! The Turanian lords fear his black arts and his power over the hybrid population, and they hate him. If he were slain in his temple at night, they would not seek his slayer very closely.'

'And what of his magic?' rumbled the Cimmerian.

'You are a fighting-man,' she answered. 'To risk your life is part of your profession.'

'For a price,' he admitted.

'There will be a price!' she breathed, rising on tiptoe, to gaze into his eyes.

The nearness of her vibrant body drove a flame through his veins. The perfume of her breath mounted to his brain. But as his arms closed about her supple figure she avoided them with a lithe movement, saying: 'Wait! First serve me in this matter.'

'Name your price.' He spoke with some difficulty.

'Pick up my lover,' she directed, and the Cimmerian stooped and swung the tall form easily to his broad shoulder. At the moment he felt as if he could have toppled over Jungir Khan's palace with equal ease. The girl murmured an endearment to the unconscious man, and there was no hypocrisy in her attitude. She obviously loved Alafdhal sincerely. Whatever business arrangement she made with Conan would have no bearing on her relationship with Alafdhal. Women are more practical about these things than men.

'Follow me!' She hurried along the street, while the Cimmerian strode easily after her, in no way discomforted by his limp burden. He kept a wary eye out for black shadows skulking under arches, but saw nothing suspicious. Doubtless the men of Darfar were all gathered at the roasting-pit. The girl turned down a narrow side street, and presently knocked cautiously at an arched door.

Almost instantly a wicket opened in the upper panel, and a black face glanced out. She bent close to the opening, whispering swiftly. Bolts creaked in their sockets, and the door opened. A giant black man stood framed against the soft glow of a copper lamp. A quick glance showed Conan the man was not from Darfar. His teeth were unfiled and his kinky hair was cropped close to his skull. He was from the Wadai.

At a word from Zabibi, Conan gave the limp body into the black's arms, and saw the young officer laid on a velvet divan. He showed no signs of returning consciousness. The blow that had rendered him senseless might have felled an ox. Zabibi bent over him for an instant, her fingers nervously twining and twisting. Then she straightened and beckoned the Cimmerian.

The door closed softly, the locks clicked behind them, and the closing wicket shut off the glow of the lamps. In the starlight of the street Zabibi took Conan's hand. Her own hand trembled a little.

'You will not fail me?'

He shook his maned head, massive against the stars.

'Then follow me to Hanuman's shrine, and the gods have mercy on our souls!'

Along the silent streets they moved like phantoms of antiquity. They went in silence. Perhaps the girl was thinking of her lover lying senseless on the divan under the copper lamps; or was shrinking with fear of what lay ahead of them in the demon-haunted shrine of Hanuman. The barbarian was thinking only of the woman moving so supplely beside him. The perfume of her scented hair was in his nostrils, the sensuous aura of her presence filled his brain and left room for no other thoughts.

Once they heard the clank of brass-shod feet, and drew into the shadows of a gloomy arch while a squad of Pelishtim watchmen swung past. There were fifteen of them; they marched in close formation, pikes at the ready, and the rearmost men had their broad brass shields slung on their backs, to protect them from a knife-stroke from behind. The skulking menace of the black man-eaters was a threat even to armed men.

As soon as the clang of their sandals had receded up the street, Conan and the girl emerged from their hiding-place and hurried on. A few moments later they saw the squat, flat-topped edifice they sought looming ahead of them.

The temple of Hanuman stood alone in the midst of a broad square, which lay silent and deserted beneath the stars. A marble wall surrounded the shrine, with a broad opening directly before the portico. This opening had no gate or any sort of barrier.

'Why don't the blacks seek their prey here?' muttered Conan. 'There's nothing to keep them out of the temple.'

He could feel the trembling of Zabibi's body as she pressed close to him.

'They fear Totrasmek, as all in Zamboula fear him, even Jungir Khan and Nafertari. Come! Come quickly, before my courage flows from me like water!'

The girl's fear was evident, but she did not falter. Conan drew his sword and strode ahead of her as they advanced through the open gateway. He knew the hideous habits of the priests of the East, and was aware that an invader of Hanuman's shrine might expect to encounter almost any sort of nightmare horror. He knew there was a good chance that neither he nor the girl would ever leave the shrine alive, but he had risked his life too many times before to devote much thought to that consideration.

They entered a court paved with marble which gleamed whitely in the starlight. A short flight of broad marble steps led up to the pillared portico. The great bronze doors stood wide open as they had stood for centuries. But no worshippers burnt incense within. In the day men and women might come timidly into the shrine and place offerings to the ape-god on the black altar. At night the people shunned the temple of Hanuman as hares shun the lair of the serpent.

Burning censers bathed the interior in a soft weird glow that created an illusion of unreality. Near the rear wall, behind the black stone altar, sat the god with his gaze fixed for ever on the open door, through which for centuries his victims had come, dragged by chains of roses. A faint groove ran from the sill to the altar, and when Conan's foot felt it, he stepped away as quickly as if he had trodden upon a snake. That groove had been worn by the faltering feet of the multitude of those who had died screaming on that grim altar.

Bestial in the uncertain light Hanuman leered with his carven mask. He sat, not as an ape would crouch, but cross-legged as a man would sit, but his aspect was no less simian for that reason. He was carved from black marble, but his eyes were rubies, which glowed red and lustful as the coals of hell's deepest pits. His great hands lay upon his lap, palms upward, taloned fingers spread and grasping. In the gross emphasis of his attributes, in the leer of his satyr-countenance, was reflected the abominable cynicism of the degenerate cult which deified him.

The girl moved around the image, making toward the back wall, and when her sleek flank brushed against a carven knee, she shrank aside and shuddered as if a reptile had touched her. There was a space of several feet between the broad back of the idol and the marble wall with its frieze of gold leaves. On either hand, flanking the idol, an ivory door under a gold arch was set in the wall.

'Those doors open into each end of a hair-pin shaped corridor,' she said hurriedly. 'Once I was in the interior of the shrine— once!' She shivered and twitched her slim shoulders at a memory both terrifying and obscene. 'The corridor is bent like a horseshoe, with each horn opening into this room. Totrasmek's chambers are enclosed within the curve of the corridor and open into it. But there is a secret door in this wall which opens directly into an inner chamber—'

She began to run her hands over the smooth surface, where no crack or crevice showed. Conan stood beside her, sword in hand, glancing warily about him. The silence, the emptiness of the shrine, with imagination picturing what might lie behind that wall, made him feel like a wild beast nosing a trap.

'Ah!' The girl had found a hidden spring at last; a square opening gaped blackly in the wall. 'Set!' she screamed, and even as Conan leaped toward her, he saw that a great misshapen hand had fastened itself in her hair. She was snatched off her feet and jerked head-first through the opening. Conan, grabbing ineffectually at her, felt his fingers slip from a naked limb, and in an instant she had vanished and the wall showed blank as before. Only from beyond it came briefly the muffled sounds of a struggle, a scream, faintly heard, and a low laugh that made Conan's blood congeal in his veins.

3 Black Hands Gripping

With an oath the Cimmerian smote the wall a terrific blow with the pommel of his sword, and the marble cracked and chipped. But the hidden door did not give way, and reason told him that doubtless it had been bolted on the other side of the wall. Turning, he sprang across the chamber to one of the ivory doors.

He lifted his sword to shatter the panels, but on a venture tried the door first with his left hand. It swung open easily, and he glared into a long corridor that curved away into dimness under the weird light of censers similar to those in the shrine. A heavy gold bolt showed on the jamb of the door, and he touched it lightly with his finger tips. The faint warmness of the metal could have been detected only by a man whose faculties were akin to those of a wolf. That bolt had been touched—and therefore drawn—within the last few seconds. The affair was taking on more and more of the aspect of a baited trap. He might have known Totrasmek would know when anyone entered the temple.

To enter the corridor would undoubtedly be to walk into whatever trap the priest had set for him. But Conan did not hesitate. Somewhere in that dim-lit interior Zabibi was a captive, and, from what he knew of the characteristics of Hanuman's priests, he was sure that she needed help badly. Conan stalked into the corridor with a pantherish tread, poised to strike right or left.

On his left, ivory, arched doors opened into the corridor, and he tried each in turn. All were locked. He had gone perhaps seventy-five feet when the corridor bent sharply to the left, describing the curve the girl had mentioned. A door opened into this curve, and it gave under his hand.

He was looking into a broad, square chamber, somewhat more clearly lighted than the corridor. Its walls were of white marble, the floor of ivory, the ceiling of fretted silver. He saw divans of rich satin, gold-worked footstools of ivory, a disk-shaped table of some massive, metal-like substance. On one of the divans a man was reclining, looking toward the door. He laughed as he met the Cimmerian's startled glare.

This man was naked except for a loin-cloth and high-strapped sandals. He was brown-skinned, with close-cropped black hair and restless black eyes that set off a broad, arrogant face. In girth and breadth he was enormous, with huge limbs on which the great muscles swelled and rippled at each slightest movement. His hands were the largest Conan had ever seen. The assurance of gigantic physical strength colored his every action and inflection.

'Why not enter, barbarian?' he called mockingly, with an exaggerated gesture of invitation.

Conan's eyes began to smolder ominously, but he trod warily into the chamber, his sword ready.

'Who the devil are you?' he growled.

'I am Baal-pteor,' the man answered. 'Once, long ago and in another land, I had another name. But this is a good name, and why Totrasmek gave it to me, any temple wench can tell you.'

'So you're his dog!' grunted Conan. 'Well, curse your brown hide, Baal-pteor, where's the wench you jerked through the wall?'

'My master entertains her!' laughed Baal-pteor. 'Listen!'

From beyond a door opposite the one by which Conan had entered there sounded a woman's scream, faint and muffled in the distance.

'Blast your soul!' Conan took a stride toward the door, then wheeled with his skin tingling. Baal-pteor was laughing at him, and that laugh was edged with menace that made the hackles rise on Conan's neck and sent a red wave of murder-lust driving across his vision.

He started toward Baal-pteor, the knuckles on his sword-hand showing white. With a swift motion the brown man threw something at him—a shining crystal sphere that glistened in the weird light.

Conan dodged instinctively, but, miraculously, the globe stopped short in midair, a few feet from his face. It did not fall to the floor. It hung suspended, as if by invisible filaments, some five feet above the floor. And as he glared in amazement, it began to rotate with growing speed. And as it revolved it grew, expanded, became nebulous. It filled the chamber. It enveloped him. It blotted out furniture, walls, the smiling countenance of Baal-pteor. He was lost in the midst of a blinding bluish blur of whirling speed. Terrific winds screamed past Conan, tugging, tearing at him, striving to wrench him from his feet, to drag him into the vortex that spun madly before him.

With a choking cry Conan lurched backward, reeled, felt the solid wall against his back. At the contact the illusion ceased to be. The whirling, titanic sphere vanished like a bursting bubble. Conan reeled upright in the silver-ceilinged room, with a gray mist coiling about his feet, and saw Baal-pteor lolling on the divan, shaking with silent laughter.

'Son of a slut!' Conan lunged at him. But the mist swirled up from the floor, blotting out that giant brown form. Groping in a rolling cloud that blinded him, Conan felt a rending sensation of dislocation—and then room and mist and brown man were gone together. He was standing alone among the high reeds of a marshy fen, and a buffalo was lunging at him, head down. He leaped aside from the ripping scimitar-curved horns, and drove his sword in behind the foreleg, through ribs and heart. And then it was not a buffalo dying there in the mud, but the brown-skinned Baal-pteor. With a curse Conan struck off his head; and the head soared from the ground and snapped beast-like tusks into his throat. For all his mighty strength he could not tear it loose—he was choking—strangling; then there was a rush and roar through space, the dislocating shock of an immeasurable impact, and he was back in the chamber with Baal-pteor, whose head was once more set firmly on his shoulders, and who laughed silently at him from the divan.

'Mesmerism!' muttered Conan, crouching and digging his toes hard against the marble.

His eyes blazed. This brown dog was playing with him, making sport of him! But this mummery, this child's play of mists and shadows of thought, it could not harm him. He had but to leap and strike and the brown acolyte would be a mangled corpse under his heel. This time he would not be fooled by shadows of illusion—but he was.

A blood-curdling snarl sounded behind him, and he wheeled and struck in a flash at the panther crouching to spring on him from the metal-colored table. Even as he struck, the apparition vanished and his blade clashed deafeningly on the adamantine surface. Instantly he sensed something abnormal. The blade stuck to the table! He wrenched at it savagely. It did not give. This was no mesmeristic trick. The table was a giant magnet. He gripped the hilt with both hands, when a voice at his shoulder brought him about, to face the brown man, who had at last risen from the divan.

Slightly taller than Conan, and much heavier, Baal-pteor loomed before him, a daunting image of muscular development. His mighty arms were unnaturally long, and his great hands opened and closed, twitching convulsively. Conan released the hilt of his imprisoned sword and fell silent, watching his enemy through slitted lids.

'Your head, Cimmerian!' taunted Baal-pteor. 'I shall take it with my bare hands, twisting it from your shoulders as the head of a fowl is twisted! Thus the sons of Kosala offer sacrifice to Yajur. Barbarian, you look upon a strangler of Yota-pong. I was chosen by the priests of Yajur in my infancy, and throughout childhood, boyhood and youth I trained in the art of slaying with the naked hands—for only thus are the sacrifices enacted. Yajur loves blood, and we waste not a drop from the victim's veins. When I was a child they gave me infants to throttle; when I was a boy I strangled young girls; as a youth, women, old men and young boys. Not until I reached my full manhood was I given a strong man to slay on the altar of Yota-pong.

'For years I offered the sacrifices to Yajur. Hundreds of necks have snapped between these fingers—' he worked them before the Cimmerian's angry eyes. 'Why I fled from Yota-pong to become Totrasmek's servant is no concern of yours. In a moment you will be beyond curiosity. The priests of Kosala, the stranglers of Yajur, are strong beyond the belief of men. And I was stronger than any. With my hands, barbarian, I shall break your neck!'

And like the stroke of twin cobras, the great hands closed on Conan's throat. The Cimmerian made no attempt to dodge or fend them away, but his own hands darted to the Kosalan's bull-neck. Baal-pteor's black eyes widened as he felt the thick cords of muscles that protected the barbarian's throat. With a snarl he exerted his inhuman strength, and knots and lumps and ropes of thews rose along his massive arms. And then a choking gasp burst from him as Conan's fingers locked on his throat. For an instant they stood there like statues, their faces masks of effort, veins beginning to stand out purply on their temples. Conan's thin lips drew back from his teeth in a grinning snarl. Baal-pteor's eyes were distended; in them grew an awful surprize and the glimmer of fear. Both men stood motionless as images, except for the expanding of their muscles on rigid arms and braced legs, but strength beyond common conception was warring there— strength that might have uprooted trees and crushed the skulls of bullocks.

The wind whistled suddenly from between Baal-pteor's parted teeth. His face was growing purple. Fear flooded his eyes. His thews seemed ready to burst from his arms and shoulders, yet the muscles of the Cimmerian's thick neck did not give; they felt like masses of woven iron cords under his desperate fingers. But his own flesh was giving way under the iron fingers of the

Cimmerian which ground deeper and deeper into the yielding throat-muscles, crushing them in upon jugular and windpipe.

The statuesque immobility of the group gave way to sudden, frenzied motion, as the Kosalan began to wrench and heave, seeking to throw himself backward. He let go of Conan's throat and grasped his wrists, trying to tear away those inexorable fingers.

With a sudden lunge Conan bore him backward until the small of his back crashed against the table. And still farther over its edge Conan bent him, back and back, until his spine was ready to snap.

Conan's low laugh was merciless as the ring of steel.

'You fool!' he all but whispered. 'I think you never saw a man from the West before. Did you deem yourself strong, because you were able to twist the heads off civilized folk, poor weaklings with muscles like rotten string? Hell! Break the neck of a wild Cimmerian bull before you call yourself strong. I did that, before I was a full-grown man—like this!'

And with a savage wrench he twisted Baal-pteor's head around until the ghastly face leered over the left shoulder, and the vertebrae snapped like a rotten branch.

Conan hurled the flopping corpse to the floor, turned to the sword again and gripped the hilt with both hands, bracing his feet against the floor. Blood trickled down his broad breast from the wounds Baal-pteor's finger nails had torn in the skin of his neck. His black hair was damp, sweat ran down his face, and his chest heaved. For all his vocal scorn of Baal-pteor's strength, he had almost met his match in the inhuman Kosalan. But without pausing to catch his breath, he exerted all his strength in a mighty wrench that tore the sword from the magnet where it clung.

Another instant and he had pushed open the door from behind which the scream had sounded, and was looking down a long straight corridor, lined with ivory doors. The other end was masked by a rich velvet curtain, and from beyond that curtain came the devilish strains of such music as Conan had never heard, not even in nightmares. It made the short hairs bristle on the back of his neck. Mingled with it was the panting, hysterical sobbing of a woman. Grasping his sword firmly, he glided down the corridor.

4 Dance, Girl, Dance!

When Zabibi was jerked head-first through the aperture which opened in the wall behind the idol, her first, dizzy, disconnected thought was that her time had come. She instinctively shut her eyes and waited for the blow to fall. But instead she felt herself dumped unceremoniously onto the smooth marble floor, which bruised her knees and hip. Opening her eyes she stared fearfully around her, just as a muffled impact sounded from beyond the wall. She saw a brown-skinned giant in a loin-cloth standing over her, and, across the chamber into which she had come, a man sat on a divan, with his back to a rich velvet curtain, a broad, fleshy man, with fat white hands and snaky eyes. And her flesh crawled, for this man was Totrasmek, the priest of Hanuman, who for years had spun his slimy webs of power throughout the city of Zamboula.

'The barbarian seeks to batter his way through the wall,' said Totrasmek sardonically, 'but the bolt will hold.'

The girl saw that a heavy golden bolt had been shot across the hidden door, which was plainly discernible from this side of the wall. The bolt and its sockets would have resisted the charge of an elephant.

'Go open one of the doors for him, Baal-pteor,' ordered Totrasmek. 'Slay him in the square chamber at the other end of the corridor.'

The Kosalan salaamed and departed by the way of a door in the side wall of the chamber. Zabibi rose, staring fearfully at the priest, whose eyes ran avidly over her splendid figure. To this she was indifferent. A dancer of Zamboula was accustomed to nakedness. But the cruelty in his eyes started her limbs to quivering.

'Again you come to me in my retreat, beautiful one,' he purred with cynical hypocrisy. 'It is an unexpected honor. You seemed to enjoy your former visit so little, that I dared not hope for you to repeat it. Yet I did all in my power to provide you with an interesting experience.'

For a Zamboulan dancer to blush would be an impossibility, but a smolder of anger mingled with the fear in Zabibi's dilated eyes.

'Fat pig! You know I did not come here for love of you.'

'No,' laughed Totrasmek, 'you came like a fool, creeping through the night with a stupid barbarian to cut my throat. Why should you seek my life?'

'You know why!' she cried, knowing the futility of trying to dissemble.

'You are thinking of your lover,' he laughed. 'The fact that you are here seeking my life shows that he quaffed the drug I gave you. Well, did you not ask for it? And did I not send what you asked for, out of the love I bear you?'

'I asked you for a drug that would make him slumber harmlessly for a few hours,' she said bitterly. 'And you—you sent your servant with a drug that drove him mad! I was a fool ever to trust you. I might have known your protestations of friendship were lies, to disguise your hate and spite.'

'Why did you wish your lover to sleep?' he retorted. 'So you could steal from him the only thing he would never give you—the ring with the jewel men call the Star of Khorala—the star stolen from the Queen of Ophir, who would pay a roomful of gold for its return. He would not give it to you willingly, because he knew that it holds a magic which, when properly controlled, will enslave the hearts of any of the opposite sex. You wished to steal it from him, fearing that his magicians would discover the key to that magic and he would forget you in his conquests of the queens of the world. You would sell it back to the queen of Ophir, who understands its power and would use it to enslave men, as she did before it was stolen.'

'And why did you want it?' she demanded sulkily.

'I understand its powers. It would increase the power of my arts.'

'Well,' she snapped, 'you have it now!'

'I have the Star of Khorala? Nay, you err.'

'Why bother to lie?' she retorted bitterly. 'He had it on his finger when he drove me into the streets. He did not have it when I found him again. Your servant must have been watching the house, and have taken it from him, after I escaped him. To the devil with it! I want my lover back sane and whole. You have the ring; you have punished us both. Why do you not restore his mind to him? Can you?'

'I could,' he assured her, in evident enjoyment of her distress. He drew a phial from among his robes. 'This contains the juice of the golden lotus. If your lover drank it he would be sane again. Yes, I will be merciful. You have both thwarted and flouted me, not once but many times; he has constantly opposed my wishes. But I will be merciful. Come and take the phial from my hand.'

She stared at Totrasmek, trembling with eagerness to seize it, but fearing it was but some cruel jest. She advanced timidly, with a hand extended, and he laughed heartlessly and drew back out of her reach. Even as her lips parted to curse him, some instinct snatched her eyes upward. From the gilded ceiling four jade-hued vessels were falling. She dodged, but they did not strike her. They crashed to the floor about her, forming the four corners of a square. And she screamed, and screamed again. For out of each ruin reared the hooded head of a cobra, and one struck at her bare leg. Her convulsive movement to evade it brought her within reach of the one on the other side and again she had to shift like lightning to avoid the flash of its hideous head.

She was caught in a frightful trap. All four serpents were swaying and striking at foot, ankle, calf, knee, thigh, hip, whatever portion of her voluptuous body chanced to be nearest to them, and she could not spring over them or pass between them to safety. She could only whirl and spring aside and twist her body to avoid the strokes, and each time she moved to dodge one snake, the motion brought her within range of another, so that she had to keep shifting with the speed of light. She could move only a short space in any direction, and the fearful hooded crests were menacing her every second. Only a dancer of Zamboula could have lived in that grisly square.

She became, herself, a blur of bewildering motion. The heads missed her by hair's breadths, but they missed, as she pitted her twinkling feet, flickering limbs and perfect eye against the blinding speed of the scaly demons her enemy had conjured out of thin air.

Somewhere a thin whining music struck up, mingling with the hissing of the serpents, like an evil night-wind blowing through the empty sockets of a skull. Even in the flying speed of her urgent haste she realized that the darting of the serpents was no longer at random. They obeyed the grisly piping of the eery music. They struck with a horrible rhythm, and perforce her swaying, writhing, spinning body attuned itself to their rhythm. Her frantic motions melted into the measures of a dance compared to which the most obscene tarantella of Zamora would have seemed sane and restrained. Sick with shame and terror Zabibi heard the hateful mirth of her merciless tormentor.

'The Dance of the Cobras, my lovely one!' laughed Totrasmek. 'So maidens danced in the sacrifice to Hanuman centuries ago—but never with such beauty and suppleness. Dance, girl, dance! How long can you avoid the fangs of the Poison People? Minutes?

Hours? You will weary at last. Your swift, sure feet will stumble, your legs falter, your hips slow in their rotations. Then the fangs will begin to sink deep into your ivory flesh—'

Behind him the curtain shook as if struck by a gust of wind, and Totrasmek screamed. His eyes dilated and his hands caught convulsively at the length of bright steel which jutted suddenly from his breast.

The music broke off short. The girl swayed dizzily in her dance, crying out in dreadful anticipation of the flickering fangs—and then only four wisps of harmless blue smoke curled up from the floor about her, as Totrasmek sprawled headlong from the divan.

Conan came from behind the curtain, wiping his broad blade. Looking through the hangings he had seen the girl dancing desperately between four swaying spirals of smoke, but he had guessed that their appearance was very different to her. He knew he had killed Totrasmek.

Zabibi sank down on the floor, panting, but even as Conan started toward her, she staggered up again, though her legs trembled with exhaustion.

'The phial!' she gasped. 'The phial!'

Totrasmek still grasped it in his stiffening hand. Ruthlessly she tore it from his locked fingers, and then began frantically to ransack his garments.

'What the devil are you looking for?' Conan demanded.

'A ring—he stole it from Alafdhal. He must have, while my lover walked in madness through the streets. Set's devils!'

She had convinced herself that it was not on the person of Totrasmek. She began to cast about the chamber, tearing up divan-covers and hangings, and upsetting vessels.

She paused and raked a damp lock of hair out of her eyes.

'I forgot Baal-pteor!'

'He's in hell with his neck broken,' Conan assured her.

She expressed vindictive gratification at the news, but an instant later swore expressively.

'We can't stay here. It's not many hours until dawn. Lesser priests are likely to visit the temple at any hour of the night, and if we're discovered here with his corpse, the people will tear us to pieces. The Turanians could not save us.'

She lifted the bolt on the secret door, and a few moments later they were in the streets and hurrying away from the silent square where brooded the age-old shrine of Hanuman.

In a winding street a short distance away Conan halted and checked his companion with a heavy hand on her naked shoulder.

'Don't forget there was a price—'

'I have not forgotten!' She twisted free. 'But we must go to—to Alafdhal first!'

A few minutes later the black slave let them through the wicket door. The young Turanian lay upon the divan, his arms and legs bound with heavy velvet ropes. His eyes were open, but they were like those of a mad dog, and foam was thick on his lips. Zabibi shuddered.

'Force his jaws open!' she commanded, and Conan's iron fingers accomplished the task.

Zabibi emptied the phial down the maniac's gullet. The effect was like magic. Instantly he became quiet. The glare faded from his eyes; he stared up at the girl in a puzzled way, but with recognition and intelligence. Then he fell into a normal slumber.

'When he awakes he will be quite sane,' she whispered, motioning to the silent slave.

With a deep bow he gave into her hands a small leathern bag, and drew about her shoulders a silken cloak. Her manner had subtly changed when she beckoned Conan to follow her out of the chamber.

In an arch that opened on the street, she turned to him, drawing herself up with a new regality.

'I must now tell you the truth,' she said. 'I am not Zabibi. I am Nafertari. And he is not Alafdhal, a poor captain of the guardsmen. He is Jungir Khan, satrap of Zamboula.'

Conan made no comment; his scarred dark countenance was immobile.

'I lied to you because I dared not divulge the truth to anyone,' she said. 'We were alone when Jungir Khan went mad. None knew of it but myself. Had it been known that the satrap of Zamboula was a madman, there would have been instant revolt and rioting, even as Totrasmek planned, who plotted our destruction.

'You see now how impossible is the reward for which you hoped. The satrap's mistress is not—cannot be for you. But you shall not go unrewarded. Here is a sack of gold.'

She gave him the bag she had received from the slave.

'Go, now, and when the sun is come up to the palace, I will have Jungir Khan make you captain of his guard. But you will take your orders from me, secretly. Your first duty will be to march a squad to the shrine of Hanuman, ostensibly to search for clues of the priest's slayer; in reality to search for the Star of Khorala. It must be hidden there somewhere. When you find it, bring it to me. You have my leave to go now.'

He nodded, still silent, and strode away. The girl, watching the swing of his broad shoulders, was piqued to note that there was nothing in his bearing to show that he was in any way chagrined or abashed.

When he had rounded a corner, he glanced back, and then changed his direction and quickened his pace. A few moments later he was in the quarter of the city containing the Horse Market. There he smote on a door until from the window above a bearded head was thrust to demand the reason for the disturbance.

'A horse,' demanded Conan. 'The swiftest steed you have.'

'I open no gates at this time of night,' grumbled the horse-trader.

Conan rattled his coins.

'Dog's son knave! Don't you see I'm white, and alone? Come down, before I smash your door!'

Presently, on a bay stallion, Conan was riding toward the house of Aram Baksh.

He turned off the road into the alley that lay between the tavern compound and the date-palm garden, but he did not pause at the gate. He rode on to the northeast corner of the wall, then turned and rode along the north wall, to halt within a few paces of the northwest angle. No trees grew near the wall, but there were some low bushes. To one of these he tied his horse, and was about to climb into the saddle again, when he heard a low muttering of voices beyond the corner of the wall.

Drawing his foot from the stirrup he stole to the angle and peered around it. Three men were moving down the road toward the palm groves, and from their slouching gait he knew they were negroes. They halted at his low call, bunching themselves as he strode toward them, his sword in his hand. Their eyes gleamed whitely in the starlight. Their brutish lust shone in their ebony faces, but they knew their three cudgels could not prevail against his sword, just as he knew it.

'Where are you going?' he challenged.

'To bid our brothers put out the fire in the pit beyond the groves,' was the sullen, guttural reply. 'Aram Baksh promised us a man, but he lied. We found one of our brothers dead in the trap-chamber. We go hungry this night.'

'I think not,' smiled Conan. 'Aram Baksh will give you a man. Do you see that door?'

He pointed to a small, iron-bound portal set in the midst of the western wall.

'Wait there. Aram Baksh will give you a man.'

Backing warily away until he was out of reach of a sudden bludgeon blow, he turned and melted around the northwest angle of the wall. Reaching his horse he paused to ascertain that the blacks were not sneaking after him, and then he climbed into the saddle and stood upright on it, quieting the uneasy steed with a low word. He reached up, grasped the coping of the wall and drew himself up and over. There he studied the grounds for an instant. The tavern was built in the southwest corner of the enclosure, the remaining space of which was occupied by groves and gardens. He saw no one in the grounds. The tavern was dark and silent, and he knew all the doors and windows were barred and bolted.

Conan knew that Aram Baksh slept in a chamber that opened into a cypress-bordered path that led to the door in the western wall. Like a shadow he glided among the trees and a few moments later he rapped lightly on the chamber door.

'What is it?' asked a rumbling voice within.

'Aram Baksh!' hissed Conan. 'The blacks are stealing over the wall!'

Almost instantly the door opened, framing the tavern-keeper, naked but for his shirt, with a dagger in his hand.

He craned his neck to stare into the Cimmerian's face.

'What tale is this—you!'

Conan's vengeful fingers strangled the yell in his throat. They went to the floor together and Conan wrenched the dagger from his enemy's hand. The blade glinted in the starlight, and blood spurted. Aram Baksh made hideous noises, gasping and gagging on a mouthful of blood. Conan dragged him to his feet and again the dagger slashed, and most of the curly beard fell to the floor.

Still gripping his captive's throat—for a man can scream incoherently even with his tongue slit—Conan dragged him out of the dark chamber and down the cypress-shadowed path, to the iron-bound door in the outer wall. With one hand he lifted the bolt and threw the door open, disclosing the three shadowy figures which waited like black vultures outside. Into their eager arms Conan thrust the innkeeper.

A horrible, blood-choked scream rose from the Zamboulan's throat, but there was no response from the silent tavern. The people there were used to screams outside the wall. Aram Baksh fought like a wild man, his distended eyes turned frantically on the Cimmerian's face. He found no mercy there. Conan was thinking of the scores of wretches who owed their bloody doom to this man's greed.

In glee the negroes dragged him down the road, mocking his frenzied gibberings. How could they recognize Aram Baksh in this half-naked, bloodstained figure, with the grotesquely shorn beard and unintelligible babblings? The sounds of the struggle came back to Conan, standing beside the gate, even after the clump of figures had vanished among the palms.

Closing the door behind him, Conan returned to his horse, mounted and turned westward, toward the open desert, swinging wide to skirt the sinister belt of palm groves. As he rode, he drew from his belt a ring in which gleamed a jewel that snared the starlight in a shimmering iridescence. He held it up to admire it, turning it this way and that. The compact bag of gold pieces clinked gently at his saddle-bow, like a promise of the greater riches to come.

'I wonder what she'd say if she knew I recognized her as Nafertari and him as Jungir Khan the instant I saw them,' he mused. 'I knew the Star of Khorala, too. There'll be a fine scene if she ever guesses that I slipped it off his finger while I was tying him with his sword-belt. But they'll never catch me, with the start I'm getting.'

He glanced back at the shadowy palm groves, among which a red glare was mounting. A chanting rose to the night, vibrating with savage exultation. And another sound mingled with it, a mad, incoherent screaming, a frenzied gibbering in which no words could be distinguished. The noise followed Conan as he rode westward beneath the paling stars.

The Vale of Lost Women (Robert E. Howard)

The thunder of the drums and the great elephant-tusk horns was deafening, but in Livia's ears the clamor seemed but a confusing muttering, dull and far away. As she lay on the angareb in the great hut, her state bordering between delirium and semi-unconsciousness.

Outward sounds and movements scarcely impinged upon her senses. Her whole mental vision, though dazed and chaotic, was yet centered with hideous certitude on the naked, writhing figure of her brother, blood streaming down his quivering thighs. Against a dim nightmare background of dusky interweaving shapes and shadows, that white form was limned in merciless and awful clarity. The air seemed still to pulsate with an agonized screaming, mingled and interwoven obscenely with a rustle of fiendish laughter.

She was not conscious of sensation as an individual, separate and distinct from the rest of the cosmos. She was drowned in a great gulf of pain—was herself but pain crystallized and manifested in flesh. So she lay without conscious thought or motion, while outside the drums bellowed, the horns clamored, and barbaric voices lifted hideous chants, keeping time to naked feet slapping the hard earth and open palms smiting one another softly.

But through her frozen mentality individual consciousness at last began slowly to seep. A dull wonder that she was still bodily unharmed first made itself manifest. She accepted the miracle without thanksgiving. The matter seemed meaningless. Acting mechanically, she sat up on the angareb and stared dully about her. Her extremities made feeble beginnings of motions, as if responding to blindly awakening nerve-centers. Her naked feet scruffed nervously at the hard-beaten dirt floor. Her fingers twitched convulsively at the skirt of the scanty under-tunic which constituted her only garment. Impersonally she remembered that once, it seemed long, long ago, rude hands had torn her other garments from her body, and she had wept with fright and shame. It seemed strange, now, that so small a wrong should have caused her so much woe. The magnitude of outrage and indignity was only relative, after all, like everything else.

The hut door opened, and a black woman entered—a lithe, pantherish creature, whose supple body gleamed like polished ebony, adorned only by a wisp of silk twisted about her strutting loins. The whites of her eyeballs reflected the firelight outside, as she rolled them with wicked meaning.

She bore a bamboo dish of food—smoking meat, roasted yams, mealies, unwieldy ingots of native bread—and a vessel of hammered gold, filled with yarati beer. These she set down on the angareb, but Livia paid no heed; she sat staring dully at the opposite wall, hung with mats woven of bamboo shoots. The young black woman laughed evilly, with a flash of dark eyes and white teeth; and with a hiss of spiteful obscenity and a mocking caress that was more gross than her language, she turned and swaggered out of the hut, expressing more taunting insolence with the motions of her hips than any civilized woman could with spoken insults. Neither the wench's words nor her actions had stirred the surface of Livia's consciousness. All her sensations were still turned inward. Still the vividness of her mental pictures made the visible world seem like an unreal panorama of ghosts and shadows. Mechanically she ate the food and drank the liquor without tasting either.

It was still mechanically that at last she rose and walked unsteadily across the hut, to peer out through a crack between the bamboos. It was an abrupt change in the timbre of the drums and horns that reacted upon some obscure part of her mind and made her seek the cause, without sensible volition.

At first she could make out nothing of what she saw; all was chaotic and shadowy, shapes moving and mingling, writhing and twisting, black formless blocks hewed out starkly against a setting of blood-red that dulled and glowed. Then actions and objects assumed their proper proportions, and she made out men and women moving about the fires. The red light glinted on silver and ivory ornaments; white plumes nodded against the glare; naked black figures strutted and posed, silhouettes carved out of darkness and limned in crimson.

On an ivory stool, flanked by giants in plumed head-pieces and leopard-skin girdles, sat a fat, squat shape, abysmal, repulsive, a toad-like chunk of blackness, reeking of the dank rotting jungle and the nighted swamps. The creature's pudgy hands rested on the sleek arch of his belly; his nape was a roll of sooty fat that seemed to thrust his bullet head forward. His eyes gleamed in the firelight, like live coals in a dead black stump. Their appalling vitality belied the inert suggestion of the gross body.

As the girl's gaze rested on that repellant figure, her body stiffened and tensed as frantic life surged through her again. From a mindless automaton, she changed suddenly to a sentient mold of live, quivering flesh, stinging and burning. Pain was drowned in hate, so intense it in turn became pain; she felt hard and brittle, as if her body were turning to steel. She felt her hate flow almost tangibly out along the line of her vision; so it seemed to her that the object of her emotion should fall dead from his carven stool because of its force.

But if Bajujh, king of Bakalah, felt any psychic discomfort because of the concentration of his captive, he did not show it. He continued to cram his frog-like mouth to capacity with handfuls of mealies scooped up from a vessel held up to him by a kneeling woman, and to stare down a broad lane which was being formed by the action of his subjects in pressing back on either hand.

Down this lane, walled with sweaty black humanity, Livia vaguely realized some important personage would come, judging from the strident clamor of drum and horn. And as she watched, one came.

A column of fighting men, marching three abreast, advanced toward the ivory stool, a thick line of waving plumes and glinting spears meandering through the motley crowd. At the head of the ebon spearmen strode a figure at the sight of which Livia started violently; her heart seemed to stop, then began to pound again, suffocatingly. Against the dusky background, this man stood out with vivid distinctness. He was clad like his followers in leopard-skin loin-clout and plumed head-piece, but he was a white man. It was not in the manner of a suppliant or a subordinate that he strode up to the ivory stool, and sudden silence fell over the throng as he halted before the squatting figure.

Livia felt the tenseness, though she only dimly knew what it portended. For a moment Bajujh sat, craning his short neck upward, like a great frog; then, as if pulled against his will by the other's steady glare, he shambled up off his stool, and stood grotesquely bobbing his shaven head.

Instantly the tension was broken. A tremendous shout went up from the massed villagers, and at a gesture from the stranger, his warriors lifted their spears and boomed a salute royale for King Bajujh. Whoever he was, Livia knew the man must indeed be powerful in that wild land, if Bajujh of Bakalah rose to greet him. And power meant military prestige—violence was the only thing respected by those ferocious races.

Thereafter Livia stood with her eyes glued to the crack in the hut wall, watching the white stranger. His warriors mingled with the

Bakalahs, dancing, feasting, swigging beer. He himself, with a few of his chiefs, sat with Bajujh and the headmen of Bakalah, cross-legged on mats, gorging and guzzling. She saw his hands dipped deep into the cooking pots with the others, saw his muzzle thrust into the beer vessel out of which Bajujh also drank. But she noticed, nevertheless, that he was accorded the respect due a king. Since he had no stool, Bajujh renounced his also, and sat on the mats with his guest. When a new pot of beer was brought, the king of Bakalah barely sipped it before he passed it to the white man. Power! All this ceremonial courtesy pointed to power—strength—prestige! Livia trembled in excitement as a breathless plan began to form in her mind.

So she watched the white man with painful intensity, noting every detail of his appearance. He was tall; neither in height nor in massiveness was he exceeded by many of the giant blacks. He moved with the lithe suppleness of a great panther. When the firelight caught his eyes, they burned like blue fire. High-strapped sandals guarded his feet, and from his broad girdle hung a sword in a leather scabbard. His appearance was alien and unfamiliar; Livia had never seen his like. But she made no effort to classify his position among the races of mankind. It was enough that his skin was white.

The hours passed, and gradually the roar of revelry lessened, as men and women sank into drunken sleep. At last Bajujh rose tottering, and lifted his hands, less a sign to end the feast, than a token of surrender in the contest of gorging and guzzling, and stumbling, was caught by his warriors who bore him to his hut. The white man rose, apparently none the worse for the incredible amount of beer he had quaffed, and was escorted to the guest hut by such of the Bakalah headmen as were able to reel along. He disappeared into the hut, and Livia noticed that a dozen of his own spearmen took their places about the structure, spears ready. Evidently the stranger was taking no chances on Bajujh's friendship.

Livia cast her glance about the village, which faintly resembled a dusky Night of Judgment, what with the straggling streets strewn with drunken shapes. She knew that men in full possession of their faculties guarded the outer boma, but the only wakeful men she saw inside the village were the spearmen about the white man's hut – and some of these were beginning to nod and lean on their spears.

With her heart beating hammer-like, she glided to the back of her prison hut and out the door, passing the snoring guard Bajujh had set over her. Like an ivory shadow she glided across the space between her hut and that occupied by the stranger. On her hands and knees she crawled up to the back of that hut. A black giant squatted here; his plumed head sunk on his knees. She wriggled past him to the wall of the hut. She had first been imprisoned in that hut, and a narrow aperture in the wall, hidden inside by a hanging mat, represented her weak and pathetic attempt at escape. She found the opening, turned sidewise, and wriggled her lithe body through, thrusting the inner mat aside.

Firelight from without faintly illumined the interior of the hut. Even as she thrust back the mat, she heard a muttered curse, felt a vise-like grasp in her hair, and was dragged bodily through the aperture and plumped down on her feet.

Staggering with the suddenness of it, she gathered her scattered wits together, and raked her disordered tresses out of her eyes, to stare up into the face of the white man who towered over her, amazement written on his dark scarred face. His sword was naked in his hand, and his eyes blazed like bale-fire, whether with anger, suspicion or surprise she could not judge. He spoke in a language she could not understand—a tongue which was not a negro guttural, yet did not have a civilized sound.

"Oh, please!" she begged. "Not so loud. They will hear..."

"Who are you?" he demanded, speaking Ophirean with a barbarous accent. "By Crom, I never thought to find a white girl in this hellish land!"

"My name is Livia," she answered. "I am Bajujh's captive. Oh, listen, please listen to me! I cannot stay here long. I must return before they miss me from my hut."

"My brother..." a sob choked her, then she continued: "My brother was Theteles, and we were of the house of Chelkus, scientists and noblemen of Ophir. By special permission of the king of Stygia, my brother was allowed to go to Kheshatta, the city of magicians, to study their arts, and I accompanied him. He was only a boy—younger than myself—" her voice faltered and broke. The stranger said nothing, but stood watching her with burning eyes, his face frowning and unreadable. There was something wild and untamable about him that frightened her and made her nervous and uncertain.

"The black Kushites raided Kheshatta," she continued hurriedly. "We were approaching the city in a camel caravan. Our guards fled and the raiders carried us away with them. But they did us no harm, and let us know that they would parley with the Stygians and accept a ransom for our return. But one of the chiefs desired all the ransom for himself, and he and his followers stole us out of the camp one night, and fled far to the south-east with us, to the very borders of Kush. There they were attacked and cut down by a band of Bakalah raiders. Theteles and I were dragged into this den of beasts—" she sobbed convulsively. "—This morning my brother was mutilated and butchered before me—"

She gagged and went momentarily blind at the memory. "They fed his body to the jackals.

How long I lay in a faint I do not know—"

Words failing her, she lifted her eyes to the scowling face of the stranger. A mad fury swept over her; she lifted her fists and beat futilely on his mighty breast, which he heeded no more than the buzzing of a fly.

"How can you stand there like a dumb brute?" She screamed in a ghastly whisper. "Are you but a beast like these others? Ah,

Mitra, once I thought there was honor in men. Now I know each has his price. You—what do you know of honor—or of mercy or decency?

You are a barbarian like the others—only your skin is white; your soul is black as theirs.

"You care naught that a man of your own color has been foully done to death by these black dogs—that a white woman is their slave! Very well." She fell back from him, panting, transfigured by her passion.

"I will give you a price," she raved, tearing away her tunic from her ivory breasts. "Am I not fair? Am I not more desirable than these soot-colored wenches? Am I not a worthy reward for blood-letting? Is not a fair-skinned virgin a price worth slaying for?

"Kill that black dog Bajujh! Let me see his cursed head roll in the bloody dust! Kill him! Kill him!" She beat her clenched fists together in the agony of her intensity. "Then take me and do as you wish with me. I will be your slave!"

He did not speak for an instant, but stood like a giant brooding figure of slaughter and destruction, fingering his hilt.

"You speak as if you were free to give yourself at your pleasure," he said, "as if the gift of your body had power to swing kingdoms. Why should I kill Bajujh to obtain you? Women are cheap as plantains in this land, and their willingness or unwillingness matters as little. You value yourself too highly. If I wanted you, I wouldn't have to fight Bajujh to take you. He would rather give you to me than to fight me."

Livia gasped. All the fire went out of her, the hut reeled dizzily before her eyes. She staggered and sank in a crumpled heap on an angareb. Dazed bitterness crushed her soul as the realization of her utter helplessness was thrust brutally upon her. The human mind clings unconsciously to familiar values and ideas, even among surroundings and conditions alien and unrelated to those environs to which such values and ideas are adapted. In spite of all Livia had experienced, she had still instinctively supposed a woman's consent the pivot point of such a game as she proposed to play. She was stunned by the realization that nothing hinged upon her at all. She could not move men as pawns in a game; she herself was the helpless pawn.

"I see the absurdity of supposing that any man in this corner of the world would act according to rules and customs existent in another corner of the planet," she murmured weakly, scarcely conscious of what she was saying, which was indeed only the vocal framing of the thought which overcame her. Stunned by the newest twist of fate, she lay motionless, until the white barbarian's iron fingers closed on her shoulder and lifted her again to her feet.

"You said I was a barbarian," he said harshly, "and that is true, Crom be thanked. If you had had men of the outlands guarding you instead of soft-gutted civilized weaklings, you would not be the slave of a black pig this night. I am Conan, a Cimmerian, and I live by the sword's edge. But I am not such a dog as to leave a white woman in the clutches of a black man; and though your kind call me a robber, I never forced a woman against her consent. Customs differ in various countries, but if a man is strong enough, he can enforce a few of his native customs anywhere. And no man ever called me a weakling!"

"If you were old and ugly as the devil's pet vulture, I'd take you away from Bajujh. simply because of the color of your hide."

"But you are young and beautiful, and I have looked at black sluts until I am sick at the guts. I'll play this game your way, simply because some of your instincts correspond with some of mine. Get back to your hut. Bajujh's too drunk to come to you tonight, and I'll see that he's occupied tomorrow. And tomorrow night it will be Conan's bed you'll warm, not Bajujh's"

"How will it be accomplished?" She was trembling with mingled emotions. "Are these all your warriors?"

"They're enough," he grunted. "Bamulas, every one of them, and suckled at the teats of war. I came here at Bajujh's request. He wants me to join him in an attack on Jihiji. Tonight we feasted. Tomorrow we hold council. When I get through with him, he'll be holding council in Hell."

"You will break the truce?"

"Truces in this land are made to be broken," he answered grimly. "He would break his truce with Jihiji. And after we'd looted the town together, he'd wipe me out the first time he caught me off guard. What would be blackest treachery in another land, is wisdom here. I have not fought my way alone to the position of war-chief of the Bamulas without learning all the lessons the black country teaches. Now go back to your hut and sleep, knowing that it is not for Bajujh but for Conan that you preserve your beauty!"

Through the crack in the bamboo wall, Livia watched, her nerves taut and trembling. All day, since their late waking, bleary and sodden, from their debauch of the night before, the black people had prepared the feast for the coming night. All day Conan the Cimmerian had sat in the hut of Bajujh, and what had passed between them, Livia could not know. She had fought to hide her excitement from the only person who entered her hut—the vindictive black girl who brought her food and drink. But that ribald wench had been too groggy from her libations of the previous night to notice the change in her captive's demeanor.

Now night had fallen again, fire lighted the village, and once more the chiefs left the king's hut and squatted down in the open space between the huts to feast and hold a final, ceremonious council. This time there was not so much beer-guzzling. Livia noticed the Bamulas casually converging toward the circle where sat the chief men. She saw Bajujh, and sitting opposite him across the eating-pots, Conan, laughing and conversing with the giant Aja, Bajujh's war-chief.

The Cimmerian was gnawing a great beef-bone, and as she watched, she saw him cast a glance across his shoulder. As if it were a signal for which they had been waiting, the Bamulas all turned their gaze toward their chief. Conan rose, still smiling, as if to reach into a near-by cooking pot—then quick as a cat he struck Aja a terrible blow with the heavy bone. The Bakalah war-chief slumped over, his skull crushed in, and instantly a frightful yell rent the skies as the Bamulas went into action like blood-mad panthers.

Cooking-pots overturned, scalding the squatting women, bamboo walls buckled to the impact of plunging bodies, screams of agony ripped the night, and over all rose the exultant "Yee! yee! yee!" of the maddened Bamulas, the flame of spears that crimsoned in the lurid glow.

Bakalah was a madhouse that reddened into a shambles. The action of the invaders paralyzed the luckless villagers by its unexpected suddenness. No thought of attack by their guests had ever entered their wooly pates. Most of the spears were stacked in the huts, many of the warriors already half-drunk. The fall of Aja was a signal that plunged the gleaming blades of the Bamulas into a hundred unsuspecting bodies; after that it was massacre.

At her peep-hole, Livia stood frozen, white as a statue, her golden locks drawn back and grasped in a knotted cluster with both hands at her temples. Her eyes were dilated, her whole body rigid. The yells of pain and fury smote her tortured nerves like a physical impact; the writhing, slashing forms blurred before her, then sprang out again with horrifying distinctness. She saw spears sink into writhing black bodies, spilling red. She saw clubs swing and descend with brutal force on kinky heads. Brands were kicked out of the fires, scattering sparks; hut-thatches smoldered and blazed up. A fresh stridency of anguish cut through the cries, as living victims were hurled headfirst into the blazing structures. The scent of scorched flesh began to sicken the air, already rank with reeking sweat and fresh blood.

Livia's overwrought nerves gave way. She cried out again and again, shrill screams of torment, lost in the roar of flames and slaughter. She beat her temples with her clenched fists. Her reason tottered, changing her cries to more awful peals of hysterical laughter. In vain she sought to keep before her the fact that it was her enemies who were dying thus horribly—that this was as she had madly hoped and plotted—that this ghastly sacrifice was but a just repayment for the wrongs done her and hers. Frantic terror held her in its unreasoning grasp.

She was aware of no pity for the victims who were dying wholesale under the dripping spears. Her only emotion was blind, stark, mad, unreasoning fear. She saw Conan, his white form contrasting with the blacks. She saw his sword flash, and men went down around him. Now a struggling knot swept around a fire, and she glimpsed a fat squat shape writhing in its midst. Conan ploughed through and was hidden from view by the twisting black figures. From the midst a thin squealing rose unbearably. The press split for an instant, and she had one awful glimpse of a reeling desperate squat figure, streaming blood. Then the throng crowded in again, and steel flashed in the mob like a beam of lightning through the dusk.

A beast-like baying rose, terrifying in its primitive exultations. Through the mob Conan's tall form pushed its way. He was striding toward the hut where the girl cowered, and in his hand he bore a ghastly relic—the firelight gleamed redly on King Bajujh's severed head. The black eyes, glassy now instead of vital, rolled up, revealing only the whites; the jaw hung slack as if in a grin of idiocy; red drops showered thickly along the ground.

Livia gave back with a moaning cry. Conan had paid the price, and was coming to claim her, bearing the awful token of his payment. He would grasp her with his hot bloody fingers, crush her lips with mouth still panting from the slaughter. With the thought came delirium. With a scream Livia ran across the hut, threw herself against the door in the back wall. It fell open, and she darted across the open space, a flitting white ghost in a realm of black shadows and red flame.

Some obscure instinct led her to the pen where the horses were kept. A warrior was just taking down the bars that separated the horse-pen from the main boma, and he yelled in amazement as she darted past him. His dusky hand clutched at her, closed on the neck of her tunic. With a frantic jerk she tore away, leaving the garment in his hand. The horses snorted and stampeded past her, rolling the black man in the dust—lean, wiry steeds of the Kushite breed, already frantic with the fire and the scent of blood.

Blindly she caught at a flying mane, was jerked off her feet, struck the ground again on her toes, sprang high, pulled and scrambled herself upon the horse's straining back. Mad with fear the herd plunged through the fires, their small hoofs knocking sparks in a blinding shower. The startled black people had a wild glimpse of the girl clinging naked to the mane of a beast that raced like the wind that streamed out his rider's loose yellow hair. Then straight for the boma the steed bolted, soared breath-takingly into the air, and was gone into the night.

Livia could make no attempt to guide her steed, nor did she feel any need of so doing. The yells and the glow of the fires were fading out behind her; the wind tossed her hair and caressed her naked limbs. She was aware only of a dazed need to hold to the flowing mane and ride, ride, ride over the rim of the world and away from all agony and grief and horror.

And for hours the wiry steed raced, until, topping a star-lit crest, he stumbled and hurled his rider headlong. She struck on soft cushioning sward, and lay for an instant half stunned, dimly hearing her mount trot away. When she staggered up, the first thing that impressed her was the silence. It was an almost tangible thing, soft, darkly velvet, after the incessant blare of barbaric horns and drums which had maddened her for days. She stared up at the great white stars clustered thickly in the dark blue sky. There was no moon, yet the starlight illuminated the land, though illusively, with unexpected clusterings of shadow. She stood on a swarded eminence from which the gently molded slopes ran away, soft as velvet under the starlight. Far away in one direction she discerned a dense dark line of trees which marked the distant forest. Here there was only night and trancelike stillness and a faint breeze blowing through the stars.

The land seemed vast and slumbering. The warm caress of the breeze made her aware of her nakedness and she wriggled uneasily, spreading her hands over her body. Then she felt the loneliness of the night, and the unbrokenness of the solitude. She was alone; she stood naked on the summit of the land and there was none to see; nothing but night and the whispering wind.

She was suddenly glad of the night and the loneliness. There was none to threaten her, or to seize her with rude violent hands. She looked before her and saw the slope falling away into a broad valley; there fronds waved thickly and the starlight reflected whitely on many small objects scattered throughout the vale. She thought they were great white blossoms, and the thought gave rise to vague memory; she thought of a valley of which the blacks had spoken with fear; a valley to which had fled the young women of a strange brown-skinned race which had inhabited the land before the coming of the ancestors of the Bakalas. There, men said, they had turned into white flowers, had been transformed by the old gods to escape their ravishers. There no black man dared to go.

But into that valley Livia dared to go. She would go down those grassy slopes which were like velvet under her tender feet; she would dwell there among the nodding white blossoms, and no man would ever come to lay hot, rude hands on her. Conan had said that pacts were made to be broken; she would break her pact with him. She would go into the vale of the lost women—she would lose herself in solitude and stillness...Even as these dreamy and disjointed thoughts floated through her consciousness, she was descending the gentle slopes, and the tiers of the valley walls were rising higher on each hand.

But so gentle were their slopes that when she stood on the valley floor, she did not have the feeling of being imprisoned by rugged walls. All about her floated seas of shadow, and great white blossoms nodded and whispered to her. She wandered at random, parting the fronds before her with her small hands, listening to the whisper of the wind through the leaves, finding a childish pleasure in the gurgling of an unseen stream. She moved as in a dream, in the grasp of a strange unreality. One thought reiterated itself continually: there she was safe from the brutality of men. She wept, but the tears were of joy. She lay full length upon the sward and clutched the soft grass as if she would crush her new-found refuge to her breast and hold it there forever.

She plucked the petals of the great white blossoms and fashioned them into a chaplet for her golden hair. Their perfume was in keeping with all other things in the valley, dreamy, subtle, enchanting.

So she came at last to a glade in the midst of the valley, and saw there a great stone, hewn as if by human hands, and adorned with ferns and blossoms and chains of flowers. She stood staring at it, and then there was movement and life about her. Turning, she saw figures stealing from the denser shadows—slender brown women, lithe, naked, with blossoms in their night-black hair. Like creatures of a dream they came about her, and they did not speak. But suddenly terror seized her as she looked into their eyes. Those eyes were luminous, radiant in the starshine; but they were not human eyes. The forms were human, but in the souls a strange change had been wrought; a change reflected in their glowing eyes. Fear descended on Livia in a wave. The serpent reared its grisly head in her new-found Paradise.

But she could not flee. The lithe brown women were all about her. One, lovelier than the rest, came silently up to the trembling girl, and enfolded her with supple brown arms. Her breath was scented with the same perfume that stole from the great white blossoms that waved in the starshine. Her lips pressed Livia's in a long terrible kiss. The Ophirean felt coldness running through her veins; her limbs turned brittle; like a white statue of marble she lay in the arms of her captress, incapable of speech or movement.

Quick, soft hands lifted her and laid her on the altar-stone amidst a bed of flowers. The brown women joined hands in a ring and moved supplely about the altar, dancing a strange dark measure. Never the sun or the moon looked on such a dance, and the great white stars grew whiter and glowed with a more luminous light as if its dark witchery struck response in things cosmic and elemental.

And a low chant arose, that was less human than the gurgling of the distant stream; a rustle of voices like the whispering of the great white blossoms that waved beneath the stars. Livia lay, conscious but without power of movement. It did not occur to her to doubt her sanity. She sought not to reason or analyze; she was and these strange beings dancing about her were; a dumb realization of existence and recognition of the actuality of nightmare possessed her as she lay helplessly gazing up at the star-clustered sky, whence, she somehow knew with more than mortal knowledge, some thing would come to her, as it had come long ago to make these naked brown women the soulless beings they now were.

First, high above her, she saw a black dot among the stars, which grew and expanded; it neared her; it swelled to a bat; and still it grew, though its shape did not alter further to any great extent. It hovered over her in the stars, dropping plummet-like earthward, its great wings spread over her; she lay in its tenebrous shadow. And all about her the chant rose higher, to a soft paean of soulless joy, a welcome to the god which came to claim a fresh sacrifice, fresh and rose-pink as a flower in the dew of dawn.

Now it hung directly over her, and her soul shrivelled and grew chill and small at the sight. Its wings were bat-like; but its body and the dim face that gazed down upon her were like nothing of sea or earth or air; she knew she looked upon ultimate horror, upon black cosmic foulness born in night-black gulfs beyond the reach of a madman's wildest dreams.

Breaking the unseen bonds that held her dumb, she screamed awfully. Her cry was answered by a deep menacing shout. She heard the pounding of rushing feet; all about her there was a swirl as of swift waters; the white blossoms tossed wildly, and the brown women were gone. Over her hovered the great black shadow, and she saw a tall white figure, with plumes nodding in the stars, rushing toward her.

"Conan!" The cry broke involuntarily from her lips. With a fierce inarticulate yell, the barbarian sprang into the air, lashing upward with his sword that flamed in the starlight.

The great black wings rose and fell. Livia, dumb with horror, saw the Cimmerian enveloped in the black shadow that hung over him. The man's breath came pantingly; his feet stamped the beaten earth, crushing the white blossoms into the dirt. The rending impact of his blows echoed through the night. He was hurled back and forth like a rat in the grip of a hound; blood splashed thickly on the sward, mingling with the white petals that lay strewn like a carpet.

And then the girl, watching that devilish battle as in a nightmare, saw the black-winged thing waver and stagger in mid-air; there was a threshing beat of crippled wings, and the monster had torn clear and was soaring upward to mingle and vanish among the stars. Its conqueror staggered dizzily, sword poised, legs wide-braced, staring upward stupidly, amazed at victory, but ready to take up again the ghastly battle.

An instant later Conan approached the altar, panting, dripping blood at every step. His massive chest heaved, glistening with perspiration. Blood ran down his arms in streams from his neck and shoulders. As he touched her, the spell on the girl was broken, and she scrambled up and slid from the altar, recoiling from his hand. He leaned against the stone, looking down at her, where she cowered at his feet.

"Men saw you ride out of the village," he said. "I followed as soon as I could, and picked up your track, though it was no easy task following it by torchlight. I tracked you to the place where your horse threw you, and though the torches were exhausted by then, and I could not find the prints of your bare feet on the sward, I felt sure you had descended into the valley. My men would not follow me, so I came alone on foot. What vale of devils is this? What was that thing?"

"A god," she whispered. "The black people spoke of it—a god from far away and long ago!"

"A devil from the Outer Dark," he grunted. "Oh, they're nothing uncommon. They lurk as thick as fleas outside the belt of light which surrounds this world. I've heard the wise men of Zamora talk of them. Some find their way to Earth, but when they do, they have to take on earthly form and flesh of some sort. A man like myself, with a sword, is a match for any amount of fangs and talons, infernal or terrestrial. Come, my men await me beyond the ridge of the valley."

She crouched motionless, unable to find words, while he frowned down at her. Then she spoke: "I ran away from you. I planned to dupe you. I was not going to keep my promise to you. I was yours by the bargain we made, but I would have escaped from you if I could. Punish me as you will."

He shook the sweat and blood from his locks, and sheathed his sword.

"Get up," he grunted. "It was a foul bargain I made. I do not regret that black dog Bajujh, but you are no wench to be bought and sold. The ways of men vary in different lands, but a man need not be a swine, wherever he is. After I thought awhile, I saw that to hold you to your bargain would be the same as if I had forced you. Besides, you are not tough enough for this land. You are a child of cities, and books, and civilized ways—which isn't your fault, but you'd die quickly following the life I thrive on. A dead woman would be no good to me. I will take you to the Stygian borders. The Stygians will send you home to Ophir."

She stared up at him as if she had not heard aright. "Home?" she repeated mechanically.

"Home? Ophir? My people? Cities, towers, peace, my home?" Suddenly tears welled into her eyes, and sinking to her knees, she embraced his knees in her arms. "Crom, girl," grunted Conan, embarrassed, "don't do that; you'd think I was doing you a favor by kicking you out of this country; haven't I explained that you're not the proper woman for the war-chief of the Bamulas?"

Red Nails *(Robert E. Howard)*

1. — THE SKULL ON THE CRAG

The woman on the horse reined in her weary steed. It stood with its legs wide-braced, its head drooping, as if it found even the weight of the gold-tassled, red-leather bridle too heavy. The woman drew a booted foot out of the silver stirrup and swung down from the gilt-worked saddle. She made the reins fast to the fork of a sapling, and turned about, hands on her hips, to survey her surroundings.

They were not inviting. Giant trees hemmed in the small pool where her horse had just drunk. Clumps of undergrowth limited the vision that quested under the somber twilight of the lofty arches formed by intertwining branches. The woman shivered with a twitch of her magnificent shoulders, and then cursed.

She was tall, full-bosomed, and large-limbed, with compact shoulders. Her whole figure reflected an unusual strength, without detracting from the femininity of her appearance. She was all woman, in spite of her bearing and her garments. The latter were incongruous, in view of her present environs. Instead of a skirt she wore short, wide-legged silk breeches, which ceased a hand's breadth short of her knees, and were upheld by a wide silken sash worn as a girdle. Flaring-topped boots of soft leather came almost to her knees, and a low-necked, wide-collared, wide-sleeved silk shirt completed her costume. On one shapely hip she wore a straight double-edged sword, and on the other a long dirk. Her unruly golden hair, cut square at her shoulders, was confined by a band of crimson satin.

Against the background of somber, primitive forest she posed with an unconscious picturesqueness, bizarre and out of place. She should have been posed against a background of sea clouds, painted masts, and wheeling gulls. There was the color of the sea in her wide eyes. And that was at it should have been, because this was Valeria of the Red Brotherhood, whose deeds are celebrated in song and ballad wherever seafarers gather.

She strove to pierce the sullen green roof of the arched branches and see the sky which presumably lay above it, but presently gave it up with a muttered oath.

Leaving her horse tied, she strode off toward the east, glancing back toward the pool from time to time in order to fix her route in her mind. The silence of the forest depressed her. No birds sang in the lofty boughs, nor did any rustling in the bushes indicate the presence of small animals. For leagues she had traveled in a realm of brooding stillness, broken only by the sounds of her own flight.

She had slaked her thirst at the pool, but now felt the gnawings of hunger and began looking about for some of the fruit on which she had sustained herself since exhausting the food originally in her saddlebags.

Ahead of her, presently, she saw an outcropping of dark, flintlike rock that sloped upward into what looked like a rugged crag rising among the trees. Its summit was lost to view amidst a cloud of encircling leaves. Perhaps its peak rose above the treetops, and from it she could see what lay beyond – if, indeed, anything lay beyond but more of this apparently illimitable forest through which she had ridden for so many days.

A narrow ridge formed a natural ramp that led up the steep face of the crag. After she had ascended some fifty feet, she came to the belt of leaves that surrounded the rock. The trunks of the trees did not crowd close to the crag, but the ends of their lower branches extended about it, veiling it with their foliage. She groped on in leafy obscurity, not able to see either above or below her; but presently she glimpsed blue sky, and a moment later came out in the clear, hot sunlight and saw the forest roof stretching away under her feet.

She was standing on a broad shelf which was about even with the treetops, and from it rose a spirelike jut that was the ultimate peak of the crag she had climbed. But something else caught her attention at the moment. Her foot had struck something in the litter of blown dead leaves which carpeted the shelf. She kicked them aside and looked down on the skeleton of a man. She ran an experienced eye over the bleached frame, but saw no broken bones nor any sign of violence. The man must have died a natural death; though why he should have climbed a tall crag to die she could not imagine.

She scrambled up to the summit of the spire and looked toward the horizons. The forest roof—which looked like a floor from her vantage point—was just as impenetrable as from below. She could not even see the pool by which she had left her horse. She glanced northward, in the direction from which she had come. She saw only the rolling green ocean stretching away and away, with just a vague blue line in the distance to hint of the hill range she had crossed days before, to plunge into this leafy waste.

West and east the view was the same, though the blue hill-line was lacking in those directions. But when she turned her eyes southward she stiffened and caught her breath. A mile away in that direction the forest thinned out and ceased abruptly, giving way to a cactus-dotted plain. And in the midst of that plain rose the walls and towers of a city. Valeria swore in amazement. This passed belief. She would not have been surprised to sight human habitations of another sort—the beehive-shaped huts of the black people, or the cliff-dwellings of the mysterious brown race which legends declared inhabited some country of this unexplored region. But it was a startling experience to come upon a walled city here so many long weeks' march from the nearest outposts of any sort of civilization.

Her hands tiring from clinging to the spirelike pinnacle, she let herself down on the shelf, frowning in indecision. She had come far—from the camp of the mercenaries by the border town of Sukhmet amidst the level grasslands, where desperate adventurers of many races guard the Stygian frontier against the raids that come up like a red wave from Darfar. Her flight had been blind, into a country of which she was wholly ignorant. And now she wavered between an urge to ride directly to that city in the plain, and the instinct of caution which prompted her to skirt it widely and continue her solitary flight.

Her thoughts were scattered by the rustling of the leaves below her. She wheeled catlike, snatched at her sword; and then she froze motionless, staring wide-eyed at the man before her.

He was almost a giant in stature, muscles rippling smoothly under his skin, which the sun had burned brown. His garb was similar to hers, except that he wore a broad leather belt instead of a girdle. Broadsword and poniard hung from his belt.

"Conan, the Cimmerian!" ejaculated the woman. "What are you doing on my trail?"

He grinned hardly, and his fierce blue eyes burned with a light any woman could understand as they ran over her magnificent figure, lingering on the swell of her splendid breasts beneath the light shirt, and the clear white flesh displayed between breeches and boot-tops.

"Don't you know?" he laughed. "Haven't I made my admiration for you plain ever since I first saw you?"

"A stallion could have made it no plainer," she answered disdainfully. "But I never expected to encounter you so far from the ale barrels and meatpots of Sukhmet. Did you really follow me from Zarallo's camp, or were you whipped forth for a rogue?"

He laughed at her insolence and flexed his mighty biceps.

"You know Zarallo didn't have enough knaves to whip me out of camp," he grinned. "Of course I followed you. Lucky thing for you, too, wench! When you knifed that Stygian officer, you forfeited Zarallo's favor, and protection, and you outlawed yourself with the Stygians."

"I know it," she replied sullenly. "But what else could I do? You know what my provocation was."

"Sure," he agreed. "If I'd been there, I'd have knifed him myself. But if a woman must live in the war camps of men, she can expect such things."

Valeria stamped her booted foot and swore.

"Why won't men let me life a man's life?"

"That's obvious!" Again his eager eyes devoured her. "But you were wise to run away. The Stygians would have had you skinned. That officer's brother followed you; faster than you thought, I don't doubt. He wasn't far behind you when I caught up with him. His horse was better than yours. He'd have caught you and cut your throat within a few more miles."

"Well?" she demanded.

"Well what?" He seemed puzzled.

"What of the Stygian?"

"Why, what do you suppose?" he returned impatiently. "I killed him, of course, and left his carcass for the vultures. That delayed me, though, and I almost lost your trail when you crossed the rocky spurs of the hills. Otherwise I'd have caught up with you long ago."

"And now you think you'll drag me back to Zarallo's camp?" she sneered.

"Don't talk like a fool," he grunted. "Come, girl, don't be such a spitfire. I'm not like that Stygian you knifed, and you know it."

"A penniless vagabond," she taunted.

He laughed at her.

"What do you call yourself? You haven't enough money to buy a new seat for your breeches. Your disdain doesn't deceive me. You know I've commanded bigger ships and more men than you ever did in your life. As for being penniless—what rover isn't, most of the time? I've squandered enough gold in the seaports of the world to fill a galeon. You know that, too."

"Where are the fine ships and the bold lads you commanded now?" she sneered.

"At the bottom of the sea, mostly," he replied cheerfully. "The Zingarans sank my last ship off the Shemite shore—that's why I joined Zarallo's Free Companions. But I saw I'd been stung when we marched to the Darfar border. The pay was poor and the wine was sour, and I don't like black women. And that's the only kind that came to our camp at Sukhmet—rings in their noses and their teeth filed—bah! Why did you join Zarallo? Sukhmet's a long way from salt water."

"Red Ortho wanted to make me his mistress," she answered sullenly. "I jumped overboard one night and swam ashore when we were anchored off the Kushite coast. Off Zabhela, it was. There was a Shemite trader told me that Zarallo had brought his Free Companies south to guard the Darfar border. No better employment offered. I joined an east-bound caravan and eventually came to Sukhmet."

"It was madness to plunge southward as you did," commented Conan, "but it was wise, too, for Zarallo's patrols never thought to look for you in this direction. Only the brother of the man you killed happened to strike your trail."

"And now what do you intend doing?" she demanded.

"Turn west," he answered. "I've been this far south, but not this far east. Many days' traveling to the west will bring us to the open savannas, where the black tribes graze their cattle. I have friends among them. We'll get to the coast and find a ship. I'm sick of the jungle."

"Then be on your way," she advised. "I have other plans."

"Don't be a fool!" He showed irratation for the first time. "You can't keep on wandering through this forest."

"I can if I choose."

"But what do you intend doing?"

"That's none of your affair," she snapped.

"Yes, it is," he answered calmly. "Do you think I've followed you this far, to turn around and ride off empty-handed? Be sensible, wench. I'm not going to harm you."

He stepped toward her, and she sprang back, whipping out her sword.

"Keep back, you barbarian dog! I'll spit you like a roast pig!"

He halted, reluctantly, and demanded: "Do you want me to take that toy away from you and spank you with it?"

"Words! Nothing but words!" she mocked, lights like the gleam of the sun on blue water dancing in her reckless eyes.

He knew it was the truth. No living man could disarm Valeria of the Brotherhood with his bare hands. He scowled, his sensations a tangle of conflicting emotions. He was angry, yet he was amused and filled with admiration for her spirit. He burned with eagerness to seize that splendid figure and crush it in his iron arms, yet he greatly desired not to hurt the girl. He was torn between a desire to shake her soundly, and a desire to caress her. He knew if he came any nearer her sword would be sheathed in his heart. He had seen Valeria kill too many men in border forays and tavern brawls to have any illusions about her. He knew she was as quick and ferocious as a tigress. He could draw his broadsword and disarm her, beat the blade out of her hand, but the thought of drawing a sword on a woman, even without intent of injury, was extremely repugnant to him.

"Blast your soul, you hussy!" he exclaimed in exasperation. "I'm going to take off your—"

He started toward her, his angry passion making him reckless, and she poised herself for a deadly thrust. Then came a startling interruption to a scene at once ludicrous and perilous.

"What's that?"

It was Valeria who exclaimed, but they both started violently, and Conan wheeled like a cat, his great sword flashing into his hand. Back in the forest had burst forth an appalling medley of screams—the screams of horses in terror and agony. Mingled with their screams there came the snap of splintering bones.

"Lions are slaying the horses!" cried Valeria.

"Lions, nothing!" snorted Conan, his eyes blazing. "Did you hear a lion roar? Neither did I! Listen to those bones snap—not even a lion could make that much noise killing a horse."

He hurried down the natural ramp and she followed, their personal feud forgotten in the adventurers' instinct to unite against common peril. The screams had ceased when they worked their way downward through the green veil of leaves that brushed the rock.

"I found your horse tied by the pool back there," he muttered, treading so noiselessly that she no longer wondered how he had surprised her on the crag. "I tied mine beside it and followed the tracks of your boots. Watch, now!"

They had emerged from the belt of leaves, and stared down into the lower reaches of the forest. Above them the green roof spread its dusky canopy. Below them the sunlight filtered in just enough to make a jade-tinted twilight. The giant trunks of trees less than a hundred yards away looked dim and ghostly.

"The horses should be beyond that thicket, over there," whispered Conan, and his voice might have been a breeze moving through the branches. "Listen!"

Valeria had already heard, and a chill crept through her veins; so she unconsciously laid her white hand on her companion's muscular brown arm. From beyond the thicket came the noisy crunching of bones and the loud rending of flesh, together with the grinding, slobbering sounds of a horrible feast.

"Lions wouldn't make that noise," whispered Conan. "Something's eating our horses, but it's not a lion—Crom!"

The noise stopped suddenly, and Conan swore softly. A suddenly risen breeze was blowing from them directly toward the spot where the unseen slayer was hidden.

"Here it comes!" muttered Conan, half lifting his sword.

The thicket was violently agitated, and Valeria clutched Conan's arm hard. Ignorant of jungle lore, she yet knew that no animal she had ever seen could have shaken the tall brush like that.

"It must be as big as an elephant," muttered Conan, echoing her thought. "What the devil—" His voice trailed away in stunned silence.

Through the thicket was thrust a head of nightmare and lunacy. Grinning jaws bared rows of dripping yellow tusks; above the yawning mouth wrinkled a saurian-like snout. Huge eyes, like those of a python a thousand times magnified, stared unwinkingly at the petrified humans clinging to the rock above it. Blood smeared the scaly, flabby lips and dripped from the huge mouth.

The head, bigger than that of a crocodile, was further extended on a long scaled neck on which stood up rows of serrated spikes, and after it, crushing down the briars and saplings, waddled the body of a titan, a gigantic, barrel-bellied torso on absurdly short legs. The whitish belly almost raked the ground, while the serrated backbone rose higher than Conan could have reached on tiptoe. A long spiked tail, like that of a gargantuan scorpion, trailed out behind.

"Back up the crag, quick!" snapped Conan, thrusting the girl behind him. "I don't think he can climb, but he can stand on his hind legs and reach us—"

With a snapping and rending of bushes and saplings, the monster came hurtling through the thickets, and they fled up the rock before him like leaves blown before a wind. As Valeria plunged into the leafy screen, a backward glance showed her the titan rearing up fearsomely on his massive hind legs, even as Conan had predicted. The sight sent panic racing through her. As he reared, the beast seemed more gigantic than ever; his snouted head towered among the trees. Then Conan's iron hand closed on her wrist and she was jerked headlong into the blinding welter of the leaves, and out again into the hot sunshine above, just as the monster fell forward with his front feet on the crag with an impact that made the rock vibrate.

Behind the fugitives the huge head crashed through the twigs, and they looked down for a horrifying instant at the nightmare visage framed among the green leaves, eyes flaming, jaws gaping. Then the giant tusks clashed together futilely, and after that the head was withdrawn, vanishing from their sight as if it had sunk in a pool.

Peering down through broken branches that scraped the rock, they saw it squatting on its haunches at the foot of the crag, staring unblinkingly up at them.

Valeria shuddered.

"How long do you suppose he'll crouch there?"

Conan kicked the skull on the leaf-strewn shelf.

"That fellow must have climbed up here to escape him, or one like him. He must have died of starvation. There are no bones broken. That thing must be a dragon, such as the black people speak of in their legends. If so, it won't leave here until we're both dead."

Valeria looked at him blankly, her resentment forgotten. She fought down a surging of panic. She had proved her reckless courage a thousand times in wild battles on sea and land, on the blood-slippery decks of burning war ships, in the storming of walled cities, and on the trampled sandy beaches where the desperate men of the Red Brotherhood bathed their knives in one another's blood in their fights for leadership. But the prospect now confronting her congealed her blood. A cutlass stroke in the heat of battle was nothing; but to sit idle and helpless on a bare rock until she perished of starvation, besieged by a monstrous survival of an elder age—the thought sent panic throbbing through her brain.

"He must leave to eat and drink," she said helplessly.

"He won't have to go far to do either," Conan pointed out. "He's just gorged on horse meat and, like a real snake, he can go for a long time without eating or drinking again. But he doesn't sleep after eating, like a real snake, it seems. Anyway, he can't climb this crag."

Conan spoke imperturbably. He was a barbarian, and the terrible patience of the wilderness and its children was as much a part of him as his lusts and rages. He could endure a situation like this with a coolness impossible to a civilized person.

"Can't we get into the trees and get away, traveling like apes through the branches?" she asked desperately.

He shook his head. "I thought of that. The branches that touch the crag down there are too light. They'd break with our weight. Besides, I have an idea that devil could tear up any tree around here by its roots."

"Well, are we going to sit here on our rumps until we starve, like that?" she cried furiously, kicking the skull clattering across the ledge. "I won't do it! I'll go down there and cut his damned head off—"

Conan had seated himself on a rocky projection at the foot of the spire. He looked up with a glint of admiration at her blazing eyes and tense, quivering figure, but, realizing that she was in just the mood for any madness, he let none of his admiration sound in his voice.

"Sit down," he grunted, catching her by her wrist and pulling her down on his knee. She was too surprised to resist as he took her sword from her hand and shoved it back in its sheath. "Sit still and calm down. You'd only break your steel on his scales. He'd gobble you up at one gulp, or smash you like an egg with that spiked tail of his. We'll get out of this jam some way, but we shan't do it by getting chewed up and swallowed."

She made no reply, nor did she seek to repulse his arm from about her waist. She was frightened, and the sensation was new to Valeria of the Red Brotherhood. So she sat on her companion's—or captor's—knee with a docility that would have amazed Zarallo, who had anathematized her as a she-devil out of Hell's seraglio.

Conan played idly with her curly yellow locks, seemingly intent only upon his conquest. Neither the skeleton at his feet nor the monster crouching below disturbed his mind or dulled the edge of his interest.

The girl's restless eyes, roving the leaves below them, discovered splashes of color among the green. It was fruit, large, darkly crimson globes suspended from the boughs of a tree whose broad leaves were a peculiarly rich and vivid green. She became aware of both thirst and hunger, though thirst had not assailed her until she knew she could not descend from the crag to find food and water.

"We need not starve," she said. "There is fruit we can reach."

Conan glanced where she pointed.

"If we ate that we wouldn't need the bite of a dragon," he grunted. "That's what the black people of Kush call the Apples of Derketa. Derketa is the Queen of the Dead. Drink a little of that juice, or spill it on your flesh, and you'd be dead before you could tumble to the foot of this crag."

"Oh!"

She lapsed into dismayed silence. There seemed no way out of their predicament, she reflected gloomily. She saw no way of escape, and Conan seemed to be concerned only with her supple waist and curly tresses. If he was trying to formulate a plan of escape he did not show it.

"If you'll take your hands off me long enough to climb up on that peak," she said presently, "you'll see something that will surprise you."

He cast her a questioning glance, then obeyed with a shrug of his massive shoulders. Clinging to the spirelike pinnacle, he stared out over the forest roof.

He stood a long moment in silence, posed like a bronze statue on the rock.

"It's a walled city, right enough," he muttered presently. "Was that where you were going, when you tried to send me off alone to the coast?"

"I saw it before you came. I knew nothing of it when I left Sukhmet."

"Who'd have thought to find a city here? I don't believe the Stygians ever penetrated this far. Could black people build a city like that? I see no herds on the plain, no signs of cultivation, or people moving about."

"How can you hope to see all that, at this distance?" she demanded.

He shrugged his shoulders and dropped down on the shelf.

"Well, the folk of the city can't help us just now. And they might not, if they could. The people of the Black Countries are generally hostile to strangers. Probably stick us full of spears—"

He stopped short and stood silent, as if he had forgotten what he was saying, frowning down at the crimson spheres gleaming among the leaves.

"Spears!" he muttered. "What a blasted fool I am not to have thought of that before! That shows what a pretty woman does to a man's mind."

"What are you talking about?" she inquired.

Without answering her question, he descended to the belt of leaves and looked down through them. The great brute squatted below, watching the crag with the frightful patience of the reptile folk. So might one of his breed have glared up at their troglodyte ancestors, treed on a high-flung rock, in the dim dawn ages. Conan cursed him without heat, and began cutting branches, reaching out and severing them as far from the end as he could reach. The agitation of the leaves made the monster restless. He rose from his haunches and lashed his hideous tail, snapping off saplings as if they had been toothpicks. Conan watched him warily from the corner of his eye, and just as Valeria believed the dragon was about to hurl himself up the crag again, the Cimmerian drew back and climbed up to the ledge with the branches he had cut. There were three of these, slender shafts about seven feet long, but not larger than his thumb. He had also cut several strands of tough, thin vine.

"Branches too light for spear-hafts, and creepers no thicker than cords," he remarked, indicating the foliage about the crag. "It won't hold our weight – but there's strength in union. That's what the Aquilonian renegades used to tell us Cimmerians when they came into the hills to raise an army to invade their own country. But we always fight by clans and tribes."

"What the devil has that got to do with those sticks?" she demanded.

"You wait and see."

Gathering the sticks in a compact bundle, he wedged his poniard hilt between them at one end. Then with the vines he bound them together and, when he had completed his task, he had a spear of no small strength, with a sturdy shaft seven feet in length.

"What good will that do?" she demanded. "You told me that a blade couldn't pierce his scales—"

"He hasn't got scales all over him," answered Conan. "There's more than one way of skinning a panther."

Moving down to the edge of the leaves, he reached the spear up and carefully thrust the blade through one of the Apples of Derketa, drawing aside to avoid the darkly purple drops that dripped from the pierced fruit. Presently he withdrew the blade and showed her the blue steel stained a dull purplish crimson.

"I don't know whether it will do the job or not," quoth he. "There's enough poison there to kill an elephant, but—well, we'll see."

Valeria was close behind him as he let himself down among the leaves. Cautiously holding the poisoned pike away from him, he thrust his head through the branches and addressed the monster.

"What are you waiting down there for, you misbegotten offspring of questionable parents?" was one of his more printable queries. "Stick your ugly head up here again, you long-necked brute—or do you want me to come down there and kick you loose from your illegitimate spine?"

There was more of it—some of it crouched in eloquence that made Valeria stare, in spite of her profane education among the seafarers. And it had its effect on the monster. Just as the incessant yapping of a dog worries and enrages more constitutionally silent animals, so the clamorous voice of a man rouses fear in some bestial bosoms and insane rage in others. Suddenly, and with appalling quickness, the mastodonic brute reared up on its mighty hind legs and elongated its neck and body in a furious effort to reach this vociferous pigmy whose clamor was disturbing the primeval silence of its ancient realm.

But Conan had judged his distance with precision. Some five feet below him the mighty head crashed terribly but futilely through the leaves. And as the monstrous mouth gaped like that of a great snake, Conan drove his spear into the red angle of the jawbone hinge. He struck downward with all the strength of both arms, driving the long poniard blade to the hilt in flesh, sinew and bone.

Instantly the jaws clashed convulsively together, severing the triple- pieced shaft and almost precipitating Conan from his perch. He would have fallen but for the girl behind him, who caught his sword-belt in a desperate grasp. He clutched at a rocky projection, and grinned his thanks back at her.

Down on the ground the monster was wallowing like a dog with pepper in its eyes. He shook his head from side to side, pawed at it, and opened his mouth repeatedly to its widest extent. Presently he got a huge front foot on the stump of the shaft and managed to tear the blade out. Then he threw up his head, jaws wide and spouting blood, and glared up at the crag with such concentrated and intelligent fury that Valeria trembled and drew her sword. The scales along his back and flanks turned from rusty brown to a dull lurid red. Most horribly the monster's silence was broken. The sounds that issued from his blood-streaming jaws did not sound like anything that could have been produced by an earthly creation.

With harsh, grating roars, the dragon hurled himself at the crag that was the citadel of his enemies. Again and again his mighty head crashed upward through the branches, snapping vainly on empty air. He hurled his full ponderous weight against the rock until it vibrated from base to crest. And rearing upright he gripped it with his front legs like a man and tried to tear it up by the roots, as if it had been a tree.

This exhibition of primordial fury chilled the blood in Valeria's veins, but Conan was too close to the primitive himself to feel anything but a comprehending interest. To the barbarian, no such gulf existed between himself and other men, and the animals, as existed in the conception of Valeria. The monster below them, to Conan, was merely a form of life differing from himself mainly in physical shape. He attributed to it characteristics similar to his own, and saw in its wrath a counterpart of his rages, in its roars and bellowings merely reptilian equivalents to the curses he had bestowed upon it. Feeling a kinship with all wild things, even dragons, it was impossible for him to experience the sick horror which assailed Valeria at the sight of the brute's ferocity.

He sat watching it tranquilly, and pointed out the various changes that were taking place in its voice and actions.

"The poison's taking hold," he said with conviction.

"I don't believe it." To Valeria it seemed preposterous to suppose that anything, however lethal, could have any effect on that mountain of muscle and fury.

"There's pain in his voice," declared Conan. "First he was merely angry because of the stinging in his jaw. Now he feels the bite of the poison. Look! He's staggering. He'll be blind in a few more minutes. What did I tell you?"

For suddenly the dragon had lurched about and went crashing off through the bushes.

"Is he running away?" inquired Valeria uneasily.

"He's making for the pool!" Conan sprang up, galvanized into swift activity. "The poison makes him thirsty. Come on! He'll be blind in a few moments, but he can smell his way back to the foot of the crag, and if our scent's here still, he'll sit there until he dies. And others of his kind may come at his cries. Let's go!"

"Down there?" Valeria was aghast.

"Sure! We'll make for the city! They may cut our heads off there, but it's our only chance. We may run into a thousand more dragons on the way, but it's sure death to stay here. If we wait until he dies, we may have a dozen more to deal with. After me, in a hurry!"

He went down the ramp as swiftly as an ape, pausing only to aid his less agile companion, who, until she saw the Cimmerian climb, had fancied herself the equal of any man in the rigging of a ship or on the sheer face of a cliff.

They descended into the gloom below the branches and slid to the ground silently, though Valeria felt as if the pounding of her heart must surely be heard from far away. A noisy gurgling and lapping beyond the dense thicket indicated that the dragon was drinking at the pool.

"As soon as his belly is full he'll be back," muttered Conan. "It may take hours for the poison to kill him—if it does at all."

Somewhere beyond the forest the sun was sinking to the horizon. The forest was a misty twilight place of black shadows and dim vistas. Conan gripped Valeria's wrist and glided away from the foot of the crag. He made less noise than a breeze blowing among the tree trunks, but Valeria felt as if her soft boots were betraying their flight to all the forest.

"I don't think he can follow a trail," muttered Conan. "But if a wind blew our body scent to him, he could smell us out."

"Mitra, grant that the wind blow not!" Valeria breathed.

Her face was a pallid oval in the gloom. She gripped her sword in her free hand, but the feel of the shagreen-bound hilt inspired only a feeling of helplessness in her.

They were still some distance from the edge of the forest when they heard a snapping and crashing behind them. Valeria bit her lip to check a cry.

"He's on our trail!" she whispered fiercely.

Conan shook his head.

"He didn't smell us at the rock, and he's blundering about through the forest trying to pick up our scent. Come on! It's the city or nothing now! He could tear down any tree we'd climb. If only the wind stays down—"

They stole on until the trees began to thin out ahead of them. Behind them the forest was a black impenetrable ocean of shadows. The ominous crackling still sounded behind them, as the dragon blundered in his erratic course.

"There's the plain ahead," breathed Valeria. "A little more and we'll—"

"Crom!" swore Conan.

"Mitra!" whispered Valeria.

Out of the south a wind had sprung up.

It blew over them directly into the black forest behind them. Instantly a horrible roar shook the woods. The aimless snapping and crackling of the bushes changed to a sustained crashing as the dragon came like a hurricane straight toward the spot from which the scent of his enemies was wafted.

"Run!" snarled Conan, his eyes blazing like those of a trapped wolf. "It's all we can do!"

Sailor's boots are not made for sprinting, and the life of a pirate does not train one for a runner. Within a hundred yards Valeria was panting and reeling in her gait, and behind them the crashing gave way to a rolling thunder as the monster broke out of the thickets and into the more open ground.

Conan's iron arm about the woman's waist half lifted her; her feet scarcely touched the earth as she was borne along at a speed she could never have attained herself. If he could keep out of the beast's way for a bit, prephaps that betraying wind would shift—but the wind held, and a quick glance over his shoulder showed Conan that the monster was almost upon them, coming like a war-galley in front of a hurricane. He thrust Valeria from him with a force that sent her reeling a dozen feet to fall in a crumpled heap at the foot of the nearest tree, and the Cimmerian wheeled in the path of the thundering titan.

Convinced that his death was upon him, the Cimmerian acted according to his instinct, and hurled himself full at the awful face that was bearing down on him. He leaped, slashing like a wildcat, felt his sword cut deep into the scales that sheathed the mighty snout—and then a terrific impact knocked him rolling and tumbling for fifty feet with all the wind and half the life battered out of him.

How the stunned Cimmerian regained his feet, not even he could have ever told. But the only thought that filled his brain was of the woman lying dazed and helpless almost in the path of the hurtling fiend, and before the breath came whistling back into his gullet he was standing over her with his sword in his hand.

She lay where he had thrown her, but she was struggling to a sitting posture. Neither tearing tusks nor trampling feet had touched her. It had been a shoulder or front leg that struck Conan, and the blind monster rushed on, forgetting the victims whose scent it had been following, in the sudden agony of its death throes. Headlong on its course it thundered until its low-hung head crashed into a gigantic tree in its path. The impact tore the tree up by the roots and must have dashed the brains from the misshapen skull. Tree and monster fell together, and the dazed humans saw the branches and leaves shaken by the convulsions of the creature they covered—and then grow quiet.

Conan lifted Valeria to her feet and together they started away at a reeling run. A few moments later they emerged into the still twilight of the treeless plain.

Conan paused an instant and glanced back at the ebon fastness behind them. Not a leaf stirred, nor a bird chirped. It stood as silent as it must have stood before Man was created.

"Come on," muttered Conan, taking his companion's hand. "It's touch and go now. If more dragons come out of the woods after us—"

He did not have to finish the sentence.

The city looked very far away across the plain, farther than it had looked from the crag. Valeria's heart hammered until she felt as if it would strangle her. At every step she expected to hear the crashing of the bushes and see another colossal nightmare bearing down upon them. But nothing disturbed the silence of the thickets.

With the first mile between them and the woods, Valeria breathed more easily. Her buoyant self-confidence began to thaw out again. The sun had set and darkness was gathering over the plain, lightened a little by the stars that made stunted ghosts out of the cactus growths.

"No cattle, no plowed fields," muttered Conan. "How do these people live?"

"Perhaps the cattle are in pens for the night," suggested Valeria, "and the fields and grazing-pastures are on the other side of the city."

"Maybe," he grunted. "I didn't see any from the crag, though."

The moon came up behind the city, etching walls and towers blackly in the yellow glow. Valeria shivered. Black against the moon the strange city had a somber, sinister look.

Perhaps something of the same feeling occurred to Conan, for he stopped, glanced about him, and grunted: "We'll stop here. No use coming to their gates in the night. They probably wouldn't let us in. Besides, we need rest, and we dont know how they'll receive us. A few hours' sleep will put us in better shape to fight or run."

He led the way to a bed of cactus which grew in a circle—a phenomenon common to the southern desert. With his sword he chopped an opening, and motioned Valeria to enter.

"We'll be safe from the snakes here, anyhow."

She glanced fearfully back toward the black line that indicated the forest some six miles away.

"Suppose a dragon comes out of the woods?"

"We'll keep watch," he answered, though he made no suggestion as to what they would do in such an event. He was staring at the city, a few miles away. Not a light shone from spire or tower. A great black mass of mystery, it reared cryptically against the moonlit sky.

"Lie down and sleep. I'll keep the first watch."

She hesitated, glancing at him uncertainly, but he sat down cross-legged in the opening, facing toward the plain, his sword across his knees, his back to her. Without further comment she lay down on the sand inside the spiky circle.

"Wake me when the moon is at its zenith," she directed.

He did not reply nor look toward her. Her last impression, as she sank into slumber, was of his muscular figure, immobile as a statue hewn out of bronze, outlined against the low-hanging stars.

2. — BY THE BLAZE OF THE FIRE JEWELS

Valeria awoke with a start, to the realization that a grey dawn was stealing over the plain.

She sat up, rubbing her eyes. Conan squatted beside the cactus, cutting off the thick pears and dexterously twitching out the spikes.

"You didn't awake me," she accused. "You let me sleep all night!"

"You were tired," he answered. "Your posterior must have been sore, too, after that long ride. You pirates aren't used to horseback."

"What about yourself?" she retorted.

"I was a kozak before I was a pirate," he answered. "They live in the saddle. I snatch naps like a panther watching beside the trail for a deer to come by. My ears keep watch while my eyes sleep."

And indeed the giant barbarian seemed as much refreshed as if he had slept the whole night on a golden bed. Having removed the thorns, and peeled off the tough skin, he handed the girl a thick, juicy cactus leaf.

"Skin your teeth in that pear. It's food and drink to a desert man. I was a chief of the Zuagirs once—desert men who live by plundering the caravans."

"Is there anything you haven't done?" inquired the girl, half in derision and half in fascination.

"I've never been king of an Hyborean kingdom," he grinned, taking an enormous mouthful of cactus. "But I've dreamed of being even that. I may be too, some day. Why shouldn't I?"

She shook her head in wonder at his calm audacity, and fell to devouring her pear. She found it not unpleasing to the palate, and full of cool and thirst-satisfying juice. Finishing his meal, Conan wiped his hands in the sand, rose, ran his fingers through his thick black mane, hitched up his sword belt and said:

"Well, let's go. If the people in that city are going to cut our throats they may as well do it now, before the heat of the day begins."

His grim humor was unconscious, but Valeria reflected that it might be prophetic. She too hitched her sword belt as she rose. Her terrors of the night were past. The roaring dragons of the distant forest were like a dim dream. There was a swagger in her stride as she moved off beside the Cimmerian. Whatever perils lay ahead of them, their foes would be men. And Valeria of the Red Brotherhood had never seen the face of the man she feared.

Conan glanced down at her as she strode along beside him with her swinging stride that matched his own.

"You walk more like a hillman than a sailor," he said. "You must be an Aquilonian. The suns of Darfar never burnt your white skin brown. Many a princess would envy you."

"I am from Aquilonia," she replied. His compliments no longer irritated her. His evident admiration pleased her. For another man to have kept her watch while she slept would have angered her; she had always fiercely resented any man's attempting to shield or protect her because of her sex. But she found a secret pleasure in the fact that this man had done so. And he had not taken advantage of her fright and the weakness resulting from it. After all, she reflected, her companion was no common man.

The sun rose up behind the city, turning the towers to a sinister crimson.

"Black last night against the moon," grunted Conan, his eys clouding with the abysmal superstition of the barbarian. "Blood-red as a threat of blood against the sun this dawn. I do not like this city."

But they went on, and as they went Conan pointed out the fact that no road ran to the city from the north.

"No cattle have trampled the plain on this side of the city," said he. "No plowshare has touched the earth for years, maybe centuries. But look: once this plain was cultivated."

Valeria saw the ancient irrigation ditches he indicated, half filled in places, and overgrown with cactus. She frowned with perplexity as her eyes swept over the plain that stretched on all sides of the city to the forest edge, which marched in a vast, dim ring. Vision did not extend beyond that ring.

She looked uneasily at the city. No helmets or spearheads gleamed on battlements, no trumpets sounded, no challenge rang from the towers. A silence as absolute as that of the forest brooded over the walls and minarets.

The sun was high above the eastern horizon when they stood before the great gate in the northern wall, in the shadow of the lofty rampart. Rust flecked the iron bracings of the mighty bronze portal. Spiderwebs glistened thickly on hinge and sill and bolted panel.

"It hasn't been opened for years!" exclaimed Valeria.

"A dead city," grunted Conan. "That's why the ditches were broken and the plain untouched."

"But who built it? Who dwelt here? Where did they go? Why did they abandon it?"

"Who can say? Maybe an exiled clan of Stygians built it. Maybe not. It doesn't look like Stygian architecture. Maybe the people were wiped out by enemies, or a plague exterminated them."

"In that case their treasures may still be gathering dust and cobwebs in there," suggested Valeria, the acquisitive instincts of her profession waking in her; prodded, too, by feminine curiosity. "Can we open the gate? Let's go in and explore a bit."

Conan eyed the heavy portal dubiously, but placed his massive shoulder against it and thrust with all the power of his muscular calves and thighs. With a rasping screech of rusty hinges the gate moved ponderously inward, and Conan straightened and drew his sword. Valeria stared over his shoulder, and made a sound indicative of surprise.

They were not looking into an open street or court as one would have expected. The opened gate, or door, gave directly into a long, broad hall which ran away and away until its vista grew indistinct in the distance. It was of heroic proportions, and the floor of a curious red stone, cut in square tiles, that seemed to smolder as if with the reflection of flames. The walls were of a shiny green material.

"Jade, or I'm a Shemite!" swore Conan.

"Not in such quantity!" protested Valeria.

"I've looted enough from the Khitan caravans to know what I'm talking about," he asserted. "That's jade!"

The vaulted ceiling was of lapis lazuli, adorned with clusters of great green stones that gleamed with a poisonous radiance.

"Green fire-stones," growled Conan. "That's what the people of Punt call them. They're supposed to be the petrified eyes of those prehistoric snakes the ancients called Golden Serpents. They glow like a cat's eyes in the dark. At night this hall would be lighted by them, but it would be a hellishly weird illumination. Let's look around. We might find a cache of jewels."

"Shut the door," advised Valeria. "I'd hate to have to outrun a dragon down this hall."

Conan grinned, and replied: "I don't believe the dragons ever leave the forest."

But he complied, and pointed out the broken bolt on the inner side.

"I thought I heard something snap when I shoved against it. That bolt's freshly broken. Rust has eaten nearly through it. If the people ran away, why should it have been bolted on the inside?"

"They undoubtedly left by another door," suggested Valeria.

She wondered how many centuries had passed since the light of outer day had filtered into that great hall through the open door. Sunlight was finding its way somehow into the hall, and they quickly saw the source. High up in the vaulted ceiling skylights were set in slot-like openings—translucent sheets of some crystalline substance. In the splotches of shadow between them, the green jewels winked like the eyes of angry cats. Beneath their feet the dully lurid floor smoldered with changing hues and colors of flame. It was like treading the floors of Hell with evil stars blinking overhead.

Three balustraded galleries ran along on each side of the hall, one above the other.

"A four-storied house," grunted Conan, "and this hall extends to the roof. It's long as a street. I seem to see a door at the other end."

Valeria shrugged her white shoulders.

"Your eyes are better than mine, then, though I'm accounted sharp-eyed among the sea-rovers."

They turned into an open door at random, and traveresed a series of empty chambers, floored like the hall, and with walls of the same green jade, or of marble or ivory or chalcedony, adorned with friezes of bronze, gold, or silver. In the ceilings the green fire-gems were set, and their light was as ghostly and illusive as Conan had predicted. Under the witch-fire glow the intruders moved like specters.

Some of the chambers lacked this illumination, and their doorways showed black as the mouth of the Pit. These Conan and Valeria avoided, keeping always to the lighted chambers.

Cobwebs hung in the corners, but there was no perceptible accumulation of dust on the floor, or on the tables and seats of marble, jade, or carnelian which occupied the chambers. Here and there were rugs of that silk known as Khitan which is practically indestructible. Nowhere did they find any windows, or doors opening into streets or courts. Each door merely opened into another chamber or hall.

"Why don't we come to a street?" grumbled Valeria. "This palace or whatever we're in must be as big as the king of Turan's seraglio."

"They must not have perished of plague," sad Conan, meditating upon the mystery of the empty city. "Otherwise we'd find skeletons. Maybe it became haunted, and everybody got up and left. Maybe—"

"Maybe, hell!" broke in Valeria rudely. "We'll never know. Look at these friezes. They portray men. What race do they belong to?"

Conan scanned them and shook his head.

"I never saw people exactly like them. But there's the smack of the East about them—Vendhya, maybe, or Kosala."

"Were you a king in Kosala?" she asked, masking her keen curiosity with derision.

"No. But I was a war chief of the Afghulis who live in the Himelian mountains above the borders of Vendhya. These people favor the Kosalans. But why should Kosalans be building a city this far to the west?"

The figures portrayed were those of slender, olive-skinned men and women, with finely chiseled, exotic features. They wore filmy robes and many delicate jeweled ornaments, and were depicted mostly in attitudes of feasting, dancing, or lovemaking.

"Easterners, all right," grunted Conan, "but from where I don't know. They must have lived a disgustingly peaceful life, though, or they'd have scenes of wars and fights. Let's go up those stairs."

It was an ivory spiral that wound up from the chamber in which they were standing. They mounted three flights and came into a broad chamber on the fourth floor, which seemed to be the highest tier in the building. Skylights in the ceiling illuminated the room, in which light the fire-gems winked pallidly. Glancing through the doors they saw, except on one side, a seies of similarly lighted chambers. This other door opened upon a balustraded gallery that overhung a hall much smaller than the one they had recently explored on the lower floor.

"Hell!" Valeria sat down disgustedly on a jade bench. "The people who deserted this city must have taken all their treasures with them. I'm tired of wandering through these bare rooms at random."

"All these upper chambers seem to be lighted," said Conan. "I wish we could find a window that overlooked the city. Let's have a look through that door over there."

"You have a look," advised Valeria. "I'm gonig to sit here and rest my feet."

Conan disappeared through the door opposite that one opening upon the gallery, and Valeria leaned back with her hands clasped behind her head, and thrust her booted legs out in front of her. These silent rooms and halls with their gleaming green clusters of ornaments and burning crimson floors were beginning to depress her. She wished they could find their way out of the maze into which they had wandered and emerge into a street. She wondered idly what furtive, dark feet had glided over those flaming floors in past centuries, how many deeds of cruelty and mystery those winking ceiling-gems had blazed down upon.

It was a faint noise that brought her out of her reflections. She was on her feet with her sword in her hand before she realized what had disturbed her. Conan had not returned, and she knew it was not he that she had heard.

The sound had come from somewhere beyond the door that opened on to the gallery. Soundlessly in her soft leather boots she glided through it, crept across the balcony and peered down between the heavy balustrades.

A man was stealing along the hall.

The sight of a human being in this supposedly deserted city was a startling shock. Crouching down behind the stone balusters, with every nerve tingling, Valeria glared down at the stealthy figure.

The man in no way resembled the figures depicted on the friezes. He was slightly above middle height, very dark, though not Negroid. He was naked but for a scanty silk clout that only partly covered his muscular hips, and a leather girdle, a hand's breadth broad, about his lean waist. His long black hair hung in lank strands about his shoulders, giving him a wild appearance. He was gaunt, but knots and cords of muscles stood out on his arms and legs, without that fleshy padding that presents a pleasing symmetry of contour. He was built with an economy that was almost repellent.

Yet it was not so much his physical appearance as his attitude that impressed the woman who watched him. He slunk along, stooped in a semi-crouch, his head turning from side to side. He grasped a wide-tipped blade in his right hand and she saw it shake with the intensity of the emotion that gripped him. He was afraid, trembling in the grip of some dire terror. When he turned his head she caught the blaze of wild eyes among the lank strands of black hair.

He did not see her. On tiptoe he glided across the hall and vanished through an open door. A moment later she heard a choking cry, and then silence fell again.

Consumed with curiosity, Valeria glided along the gallery until she came to a door above the one through which the man had passed. It opened into another, smaller gallery that encircled a large chamber.

This chamber was on the third floor, and its ceiling was not so high as that of the hall. It was lighted only by the fire-stones, and their weird green glow left the spaces under the balcony in shadows.

Valeria's eyes widened. The man she had seen was still in the chamber.

He lay face down on a dark crimson carpet in the middle of the room. His body was limp, his arms spread wide. His curved sword lay near him.

She wondered why he should lie there so motionless. Then her eyes narrowed as she stared down at the rug on which he lay. Beneath and about him the fabric showed a slightly different color, a deeper, brighter crimson.

Shivering slightly, she crouched down closer behind the balustrade, intently scanning the shadows under the overhanging gallery. They gave up no secret.

Suddenly another figure entered the grim drama. He was a man similar to the first, and he came in by a door opposite that which gave upon the hall.

His eyes glared at the sight of the man on the floor, and he spoke something in a staccato voice that sounded like "Chicmec!" The other did not move.

The man stepped quickly across the floor, bent, gripped the fallen man's shoulder and turned him over. A choking cry escaped him as the head fell back limply, disclosing a throat that had been severed from ear to ear.

The man let the corpse fall back upon the blood-stained carpet, and sprang to his feet, shaking like a windblown leaf. His face was an ashy mask of fear. But with one knee flexed for flight, he froze suddenly, became as immobile as an image, staring across the chamber with dilated eyes.

In the shadows beneath the balcony a ghostly light began to glow and grow, a light that was not part of the fire-stone gleam. Valeria felt her hair stir as she watched it; for, dimly visible in the throbbing radiance, there floated a human skull, and it was from this skull—human yet appallingly misshapen—that the spectral light seemed to emanate. It hung there like a disembodied head, conjured out of night and the shadows, growing more and more distinct; human, and yet not human as she knew humanity.

The man stood motionless, an embodiment of paralyzed horror, staring fixedly at the apparition. The thing moved out from the wall and a grotesque shadow moved with it. Slowly the shadow became visible as a man-like figure whose naked torso and limbs shone whitely, with the hue of bleached bones. The bare skull on its shoulders grinned eyelessly, in the midst of its unholy nimbus, and the man confronting it seemed unable to take his eyes from it. He stood still, his sword dangling from nerveless fingers, on his face the expression of a man bound by the spells of a mesmerist.

Valeria realized that it was not fear alone that paralyzed him. Some hellish quality of that throbbing glow had robbed him of his power to think and act. She herself, safely above the scene, felt the subtle impact of a nameless emanation that was a threat to sanity.

The horror swept toward its victim and he moved at last, but only to drop his sword and sink to his knees, covering his eyes with his hands. Dumbly he awaited the stroke of the blade that now gleamed in the apparition's hand as it reared above him like Death triumphant over mankind.

Valeria acted according to the first impulse of her wayward nature. With one tigerish movement she was over the balustrade and dropping to the floor behind the awful shape. It wheeled at the thud of her soft boots on the floor, but even as it turned, her keen blade lashed down and a fierce exultation swept her as she felt the edge cleave solid flesh and mortal bone.

The apparition cried out gurglingly and went down, severed through the shoulder, breastbone and spine, and as it fell the burning skull rolled clear, revealing a lank mop of black hair and a dark face twisted in the convulsions of death. Beneath the horrific masquerade there was a human being, a man similar to the one kneeling supinely on the floor.

The latter looked up at the sound of the blow and the cry, and now he glared in wild-eyed amazement at the white-skinned woman who stood over the corpse with a dripping sword in her hand.

He staggered up, yammering as if the sight had almost unseated his reason. She was amazed to realize that she understood him. He was gibbering in the Stygian tongue, though in a dialect unfamiliar to her.

"Who are you? Whence come you? What do you in Xuchotl?" Then rushing on, without waiting for her to reply: "But you are a friend—goddess or devil, it makes no difference! You have slain the Burning Skull! It was but a man beneath it, after all! We deemed it a demon they conjured up out of the catacombs! Listen!"

He stopped short in his ravings and stiffened, straining his ears with painful intensity. The girl heard nothing.

"We must hasten!" he whispered. "They are west of the Great Hall! They may be all around us here! They may be creeping upon us even now!"

He seized her wrist in a convulsive grasp she found hard to break.

"Whom do you mean by 'they?'" she demanded.

He stared at her uncomprehendingly for an instant, as if he found her ignorance hard to understand.

"They?" he stammered vaguely. "Why—why, the people of Xotalanc! The clan of the man you slew. They who dwell by the eastern gate."

"You mean to say this city is inhabited?" she exclaimed.

"Aye! Aye!" He was writhing in the impatience of apprehension. "Come away! Come quick! We must return to Tecuhltli!"

"Where is that?" she demanded.

"The quarter by the western gate!" He had her wrist again and was pulling her toward the door through which he had first come. Great beads of perspiration dripped from his dark forehead, and his eyes blazed with terror.

"Wait a minute!" she growled, flinging off his hand. "Keep your hands off me, or I'll split your skull. What's all this about? Who are you? Where would you take me?"

He took a firm grip on himself, casting glances to all sides, and began speaking so fast his words tripped over each other.

"My name is Techotl. I am of Techultli. I and this man who lies with his throat cut came into the Halls of Silence to try and ambush some of the Xotalancas. But we became separated and I returned here to find him with his gullet slit. The Burning Skull did it, I know, just as he would have slain me had you not killed him. But perhaps he was not alone. Others may be stealing from Xotalanc! The gods themselves blench at the fate of those they take alive!"

At the thought he shook as with an ague and his dark skin grew ashy. Valeria frowned puzzledly at him. She sensed intelligence behind this rigmarole, but it was meaningless to her.

She turned toward the skull, which still glowed and pulsed on the floor, and was reaching a booted toe tentatively toward it, when the man who called himself Techotl sprang forward with a cry.

"Do not touch it! Do not even look at it! Madness and death lurk in it. The wizards of Xotalanc understand its secret—they found it in the catacombs, where lie the bones of terrible kings who ruled in Xuchotl in the black centuries of the past. To gaze upon it freezes the blood and withers the brain of a man who understands not its mystery. To touch it causes madness and destruction."

She scowled at him uncertainly. He was not a reassuring figure, with his lean, muscle-knotted frame, and snaky locks. In his eyes, behind the glow of terror, lurked a weird light she had never seen in the eyes of a man wholly sane. Yet he seemed sincere in his protestations.

"Come!" he begged, reaching for her hand, and then recoiling as he remembered her warning. "You are a stranger. How you came here I do not know, but if you were a goddess or a demon, come to aid Tecuhltli, you would know all the things you have asked me. You must be from beyond the great forest, whence our ancestors came. But you are our friend, or you would not have slain my enemy. Come quickly, before the Xotalancas find us and slay us!"

From his repellent, impassioned face she glanced to the sinister skull, smoldering and glowing on the floor near the dead man. It was like a skull seen in a dream, undeniably human, yet with disturbing distortions and malformations of contour and outline. In life the wearer of that skull must have presented an alien and monstrous aspect. Life? It seemed to possess some sort of life of its own. Its jaws yawned at her and snapped together. Its radiance grew brighter, more vivid, yet the impression of nightmare grew too; it was a dream; all life was a dream—it was Techotl's urgent voice which snapped Valeria back from the dim gulfs whither she was drifting.

"Do not look at the skull! Do not look at the skull!" It was a far cry from across unreckoned voids.

Valeria shook herself like a lion shaking his mane. Her vision cleared. Techotl was chattering: "In life it housed the awful brain of a king of magicians! It holds still the life and fire of magic drawn from outer spaces!"

With a curse Valeria leaped, lithe as a panther, and the skull crashed to flaming bits under her swinging sword. Somewhere in the room, or in the void, or in the dim reaches of her consciousness, an inhuman voice cried out in pain and rage.

Techotl's hand was plucking at her arm and he was gibbering: "You have broken it! You have destroyed it! Not all the black arts of Xotalanc can rebuild it! Come away! Come away quickly, now!"

"But I can't go," she protested. "I have a friend somewhere near by—"

The flare of his eyes cut her short as he stared past her with an expression grown ghastly. She wheeled just as four men rushed through as many doors, converging on the pair in the center of the chamber.

They were like the others she had seen, the same knotted muscles bulging on otherwise gaunt limbs, the same lank blue-black hair, the same mad glare in their wild eyes. They were armed and clad like Techotl, but on the breast of each was painted a white skull.

There were no challenges or war cries. Like blood-mad tigers the men of Xotalanc sprang at the throats of their enemies. Techotl met them with the fury of desperation, ducked the swipe of a wide-headed blade, and grappled with the wielder, and bore him to the floor where they rolled and wrestled in murderous silence.

The other three swarmed on Valeria, their weird eyes red as the eyes of mad dogs.

She killed the first who came within reach before he could strike a blow, her long straight blade splitting his skull even as his own sword lifted for a stroke. She side-stepped a thrust, even as she parried a slash. Her eyes danced and her lips smiled without mercy. Again she was Valeria of the Red Brotherhood, and the hum of her steel was like a bridal song in her ears.

Her sword darted past a blade that sought to parry, and sheathed six inches of its point in a leather-guarded midriff. The man gasped agonizedly and went to his knees, but his tall mate lunged in, in ferocious silence, raining blow on blow so furiously that Valeria had no opportunity to counter. She stepped back coolly, parrying the strokes and watching for her chance to thrust home. He could not long keep up that flailing whirlwind. His arm would tire, his wind would fail; he would weaken, falter, and then her blade would slide smoothly into his heart. A sidelong glance showed her Techotl kneeling on the breast of his antagonist and striving to break the other's hold on his wrist and to drive home a dagger.

Sweat beaded the forehead of the man facing her, and his eyes were like burning coals. Smite as he would, he could not break past nor beat down her guard. His breath came in gusty gulps, his blows began to fall erratically. She stepped back to draw him out—and felt her thighs locked in an iron grip. She had forgotten the wounded man on the floor.

Crouching on his knees, he held her with both arms locked about her legs, and his mate croaked in triumph and began working his way around to come at her from the left side. Valeria wrenched and tore savagely, but in vain. She could free herself of this clinging menace with a downward flick of her sword, but in that instant the curved blade of the tall warrior would crash through her skull. The wounded man began to worry at her bare thigh with his teeth like a wild beast.

She reached down with her left hand and gripped his long hair, forcing his head back so that his white teeth and rolling eyes gleamed up at her. The tall Xotalanc cried out fiercely and leaped in, smiting with all the fury of his arm. Awkwardly she parried the stroke, and it beat the flat of her blade down on her head so that she saw sparks flash before her eyes, and staggered. Up went the sword again, with a low, beast-like cry of triumph—and then a giant form loomed behind the Xotalanc and steel flashed like a jet of blue lightning. The cry of the warrior broke short and he went down like an ox beneath the pole-ax, his brains gushing from his skull that had been split to the throat.

"Conan!" gasped Valeria. In a gust of passion she turned on the Xotalanc whose long hair she still gripped in her left hand. "Dog of hell!" Her blade swished as it cut the air in an upswinging arc with a blur in the middle, and the headless body slumped down, spurting blood. She hurled the severed head across the room.

"What the devil's going on here?" Conan bestrode the corpse of the man he had killed, broadsword in hand, glaring about him in amazement.

Techotl was rising from the twitching figure of the last Xotalanc, shaking red drops from his dagger. He was bleeding from the stab deep in the thigh. He stared at Conan with dilated eyes.

"What is all this?" Conan demanded again, not yet recovered from the stunning surprise of finding Valeria engaged in a savage battle with fantastic figures in a city he had thought empty and uninhabited. Returning from an aimless exploration of the upper chambers to find Valeria missing from the room where he had left her, he had followed the sounds of strife that burst on his dumfounded ears.

"Five dead dogs!" exclaimed Techotl, his flaming eyes reflecting a ghastly exultation. "Five slain! Five crimson nails for the black pillar! The gods of blood be thanked!"

He lifted quivering hands on high, and then, with the face of a fiend, he spat on the corpses and stamped on their faces, dancing in his ghoulish glee. His recent allies eyed him in amazement, and Conan asked, in the Aquilonian tongue: "Who is this madman?"

Valeria shrugged her shoulders.

"He says his name's Techotl. From his babblings I gather that his people live at one end of this crazy city, and these others at the other end. Maybe we'd better go with him. He seems friendly, and it's easy to see that the other clan isn't."

Techotl had ceased his dancing and was listening again, his head tilted sidewise, dog-like, triumph struggling with fear in his repellent countenance.

"Come away, now!" he whispered. "We have done enough! Five dead dogs! My people will welcome you! They will honor you! But come! It is far to Tecuhltli. At any moment the Xotalancs may come on us in numbers too great even for your swords."

"Lead the way," grunted Conan.

Techotl instantly mounted a stair leading up to the gallery, beckoning them to follow him, which they did, moving rapidly to keep on his heels. Having reached the gallery, he plunged into a door that opened toward the west, and hurried through chamber after chamber, each lighted by skylights or green fire-jewels.

"What sort of place can this be?" muttered Valeria under her breath.

"Crom knows!" answered Conan. "I've seen his kind before, though. They live on the shores of Lake Zuad, near the border of Kush. They're a sort of mongrel Stygians, mixed with another race that wandered into Stygia from the east some centuries ago and were absorbed by them. They're called Tlazitlans. I'm willing to bet it wasn't they who built this city, though."

Techotl's fear did not seem to diminish as they drew away from the chamber where the dead men lay. He kept twisting his head on his shoulder to listen for sounds of pursuit, and stared with burning intensity into every doorway they passed.

Valeria shivered in spite of herself. She feared no man. But the weird floor beneath her feet, the uncanny jewels over her head, dividing the lurking shadows among them, the stealth and terror of their guide, impressed her with a nameless apprehension, a sensation of lurking, inhuman peril.

"They may be between us and Tecuhltli!" he whispered once. "We must beware lest they be lying in wait!"

"Why don't we get out of this infernal palace, and take to the streets?" demanded Valeria.

"There are no streets in Xuchotl," he answered. "No squares nor open courts. The whole city is built like one giant palace under one great roof. The nearest approach to a street is the Great Hall which traverses the city from the north gate to the south gate. The only doors opening into the outer world are the city gates, through which no living man has passed for fifty years."

"How long have you dwelt here?" asked Conan.

"I was born in the castle of Tecuhltli thirty-five years ago. I have never set foot outside the city. For the love of the gods, let us go silently! These halls may be full of lurking devils. Olmec shall tell you all when we reach Tecuhltli."

So in silence they glided on with the green fire-stones blinking overhead and the flaming floors smoldering under their feet, and it seemed to Valeria as if they fled through Hell, guided by a dark-faced lank-haired goblin.

Yet it was Conan who halted them as they were crossing an unusually wide chamber. His wilderness-bred ears were keener even than the ears of Techotl, whetted though these were by a lifetime of warfare in these silent corridors.

"You think some of your enemies may be ahead of us, lying in ambush?"

"They prowl through these rooms at all hours," answered Techotl, "as do we. The halls and chambers between Tecuhltli and Xotalanc are a disputed region, owned by no man. We call it the Halls of Silence. Why do you ask?"

"Because men are in the chambers ahead of us," answered Conan. "I heard steel clink against stone."

Again a shaking seized Techotl, and he clenched his teeth to keep them from chattering.

"Perhaps they are your friends," suggested Valeria.

"We dare not chance it," he panted, and moved with frenzied activity. He turned aside and glided through a doorway on the left which led into a chamber from which an ivory staircase wound down into darkness.

"This leads to an unlighted corridor below us!" he hissed, great beads of perspiration standing out on his brow. "They may be lurking there, too. It may all be a trick to draw us into it. But we must take the chance that they have laid their ambush in the rooms above. Come swiftly now!"

Softly as phantoms they descended the stair and came to the mouth of a corridor black as night. They crouched there for a moment, listening, and then melted into it. As they moved along, Valeria's flesh crawled between her shoulders in momentary expectation of a sword-thrust in the dark. But for Conan's iron fingers gripping her arm she had no physical cognizance of her companions. Neither made as much noise as a cat would have made. The darkness was absolute. One hand, outstretched, touched a wall, and occasionally she felt a door under her fingers. The hallway seemed interminable.

Suddenly they were galvanized by a sound behind them. Valeria's flesh crawled anew, for she recognized it as the soft opening of a door. Men had come into the corridor behind them. Even with the thought she stumbled over something that felt like a human skull. It rolled across the floor with an appalling clatter.

"Run!" yelped Techotl, a note of hysteria in his voice, and was away down the corridor like a flying ghost.

Again Valeria felt Conan's hand bearing her up and sweeping her along as they raced after their guide. Conan could see in the dark no better than she, but he possessed a sort of instinct that made his course unerring. Without his support and guidance she would have fallen or stumbled against the wall. Down the corridor they sped, while the swift patter of flying feet drew closer and closer, and then suddenly Techotl panted: "Here is the stair! After me, quick! Oh, quick!"

His hand came out of the dark and caught Valeria's wrist as she stumbled blindly on the steps. She felt herself half dragged, half lifted up the winding stair, while Conan released her and turned on the steps, his ears and instincts telling him their foes were hard at their backs. And the sounds were not all those of human feet.

Something came writhing up the steps, something that slithered and rustled and brought a chill in the air with it. Conan lashed down with his great sword and felt the blade shear through something that might have been flesh and bone, and cut deep into the stair beneath. Something touched his foot that chilled like the touch of frost, and then the darkness beneath him was disturbed by a frightful thrashing and lashing, and a man cried out in agony.

The next moment Conan was racing up the winding staircase, and through a door that stood open at the head.

Valeria and Techotl were already through, and Techotl slammed the door and shot a bolt across it—the first Conan had seen since they had left the outer gate.

Then he turned and ran across the well-lighted chamber into which they had come, and as they passed through the farther door, Conan glanced back and saw the door groaning and straining under heavy pressure violently applied from the other side.

Though Techotl did not abate either his speed or his caution, he seemed more confident now. He had the air of a man who had come into familiar territory, within call of friends.

But Conan renewed his terror by asking: "What was that thing I fought on the stairs?"

"The men of Xotalanc," answered Techotl, without looking back. "I told you the halls were full of them."

"This wasn't a man," grunted Conan. "It was something that crawled, and it was as cold as ice to the touch. I think I cut it asunder. It fell back on the men who were following us, and must have killed one of them in its death throes."

Techotl's head jerked back, his face ashy again. Convulsively he quickened his pace.

"It was the Crawler! A monster they have brought out of the catacombs to aid them! What it is, we do not know, but we have found our people hideously slain by it. In Set's name, hasten! If they put it on our trail, it will follow us to the very doors of Tecuhltli!"

"I doubt it," grunted Conan. "That was a shrewd cut I dealt it on the stair."

"Hasten! Hasten!" groaned Techotl.

They ran through a series of green-lit chambers, traversed a broad hall, and halted before a giant bronze door.

Techotl said: "This is Tecuhltli!"

3. — THE PEOPLE OF THE FEUD

TECHOTL smote on the bronze door with his clenched hand, and then turned sidewise, so that he could watch back along the hall.

"Men have been smitten down before this door, when they thought they were safe," he said.

"Why don't they open the door?" asked Conan.

"They are looking at us through the Eye," answered Techotl. "They are puzzled at the sight of you." He lifted his voice and called: "Open the door, Excelan! It is I, Techotl, with friends from the great world beyond the forest! – They will open," he assured his allies.

"They'd better do it in a hurry, then," said Conan grimly. "I hear something crawling along the floor beyond the hall."

Techotl went ashy again and attacked the door with his fists, screaming: "Open, you fools, open! The Crawler is at our heels!"

Even as he beat and shouted, the great bronze door swung noiselessly back, revealing a heavy chain across the entrance, over which spearheads bristled and fierce countenances regarded them intently for an instant. Then the chain was dropped and Techotl grasped the arms of his friends in a nervous frenzy and fairly dragged them over the threshold. A glance over his shoulder just as the door was closing showed Conan the long dim vista of the hall, and dimly framed at the other end an ophidian shape that writhed slowly and painfully into view, flowing in a dull-hued length from a chamber door, its hideous bloodstained head wagging drunkenly. Then the closing door shut off the view.

Inside the square chamber into which they had come heavy bolts were drawn across the foor, and the chain locked into place. The door was made to stand the battering of a siege. Four men stood on guard, of the same lank-haired, dark-skinned breed as Techotl, with spears in their hands and swords at their hips. In the wall near the door there was a complicated contrivance of mirrors which Conan guessed was the Eye Techotl had mentioned, so arranged that a narrow, crystal-paned slot in the wall could be looked through from within without being discernible from without. The four guardsmen stared at the strangers with wonder, but asked no question, nor did Techotl vouchsafe any information. He moved with easy confidence now, as if he had shed his cloak of indecision and fear the instant he crossed the threshold.

"Come!" he urged his new-found friends, but Conan glanced toward the door.

"What about those fellows who were following us? Won't they try to storm that door?"

Techotl shook his head.

"They know they cannot break down the Door of the Eagle. They will flee back to Xotalanc, with their crawling fiend. Come! I will take you to the rulers of Tecuhltli."

One of the four guards opened the door opposite the one by which they had entered, and they passed through into a hallway which, like most of the rooms on that level, was lighted by both the slot-like skylights and the clusters of winking fire-gems. But unlike the other rooms they had traversed, this hall showed evidences of occupation. Velvet tapestries adorned the glossy jade walls, rich rugs were on the crimson floors, and the ivory seats, benches and divans were littered with satin cushions.

The hall ended in an ornate door, before which stood no guard. Without ceremony Techotl thrust the door open and ushered his friends into a broad chamber, where some thirty dark-skinned men and women lounged on satin-covered couches and sprang up with exclamations of amazement.

The men, all except one, were of the same type as Techotl, and the women were equally dark and strange-eyed, though not unbeautiful in a weird dark way. They wore sandals, golden breastplates, and scanty silk skirts supported by gem-crusted girdles, and their black manes, cut square at their naked shoulders, were bound with silver circlets.

On a wide ivory seat on a jade dais sat a man and a woman who differed subtly from the others. He was a giant, with an enormous sweep of breast and the shoulders of a bull. Unlike the others, he was bearded, with a thick, blue-black beard which fell almost to his broad girdle. He wore a robe of purple silk which reflected changing sheens of color with his every movement, and one wide sleeve, drawn back to his elbow, revealed a forearm massive with corded muscles. The band which confined his blue-black locks was set with glittering jewels.

The woman beside him sprang to her feet with a startled exclamation as the strangers entered, and her eyes, passing over Conan, fixed themselves with burning intensity on Valeria. She was tall and lithe, by far the most beautiful woman in the room.

She was clad more scantily even than the others; for instead of a skirt she wore merely a broad strip of gilt-worked purple cloth fastened to the middle of her girdle which fell below her knees. Another strip at the back of her girdle completed that part of her costume, which she wore with a cynical indifference. Her breast-plates and the circlet about her temples were adorned with gems. In her eyes alone of all the dark-skinned people there lurked no brooding gleam of madness. She spoke no word after her first exclamation; she stood tensely, her hands clenched, staring at Valeria.

The man on the ivory seat had not risen.

"Prince Olmec," spoke Techotl, bowing low, with arms outspread and the palms of his hands turned upward, "I bring allies from the world beyond the forest. In the Chamber of Tezcoti the Burning Skull slew Chicmec, my companion—"

"The Burning Skull!" It was a shuddering whisper of fear from the people of Tecuhltli.

"Aye! Then came I, and found Chicmec lying with his throat cut. Before I could flee, the Burning Skull came upon me, and when I looked upon it my blood became as ice and the marrow of my bones melted. I could neither fight nor run. I could only await the stroke. Then came this white-skinned woman and struck him down with her sword; and lo, it was only a dog of Xotalanc with white paint upon his skin and the living skull of an ancient wizard upon his head! Now that skull lies in many pieces, and the dog who wore it is a dead man!"

An indescribably fierce exultation edged the last sentence, and was echoed in the low, savage exclamations from the crowding listeners.

"But wait!" exclaimed Techotl. "There is more! While I talked with the woman, four Xotalancs came upon us! One I slew— there is the stab in my thigh to prove how desperate was the fight. Two the woman killed. But we were hard pressed when this man came into the fray and split the skull of the fourth! Aye!

Five crimson nails there are to be driven into the pillar of vengeance!"

He pointed to a black column of ebony which stood behind the dais. Hundreds of red dots scarred its polished surface—the bright scarlet heads of heavy copper nails driven into the black wood.

"Five red nails for five Xotalanca lives!" exulted Techotl, and the horrible exultation in the faces of the listeners made them inhuman.

"Who are these people?" asked Olmec, and his voice was like the low, deep rumble of a distant bull. None of the people of Xuchotl spoke loudly. It was as if they had absorbed into their souls the silence of the empty halls and deserted chambers.

"I am Conan, a Cimmerian," answered the barbarian briefly. "This woman is Valeria of the Red Brotherhood, an Aquilonian pirate. We are deserters from an army on the Darfar border, far to the north, and are trying to reach the coast."

The woman on the dais spoke loudly, her words tripping in her haste.

"You can never reach the coast! There is no escape from Xuchotl! You will spend the rest of your lives in this city!"

"What do you mean," growled Conan, clapping his hand to his hilt and stepping about so as to face both the dais and the rest of the room. "Are you telling us we're prisoners?"

"She did not mean that," interposed Olmec. "We are your friends. We would not restrain you against your will. But I fear other circumstances will make it impossible for you to leave Xuchotl."

His eyes flickered to Valeria, and he lowered them quickly.

"This woman is Tascela," he said. "She is a princess of Tecuhltli. But let food and drink be brought our guests. Doubtless they are hungry, and weary from their long travels."

He indicated an ivory table, and after an exchange of glances, the adventurers seated themselves. The Cimmerian was suspicious. His fierce blue eyes roved about the chamber, and he kept his sword close to his hand. But an invitation to eat and drink never found him backward. His eyes kept wandering to Tascela, but the princess had eyes only for his white-skinned companion.

Techotl, who had bound a strip of silk about his wounded thigh, placed himself at the table to attend to the wants of his friends, seeming to consider it a privilege and honor to see after their needs. He inspected the food and drink the others brought in gold vessels and dishes, and tasted each before he placed it before his guests. While they ate, Olmec sat in silence on his ivory seat, watching them from under his broad black brows. Tascela sat beside him, chin cupped in her hands and her elbows resting on her knees. Her dark, enigmatic eyes, burning with a mysterious light, never left Valeria's supple figure. Behind her seat a sullen handsome girl waved an ostrich-plume fan with a slow rhythm.

The food was fruit of an exotic kind unfamiliar to the wanderers, but very palatable, and the drink was a light crimson wine that carried a heady tang.

"You have come from afar," said Olmec at last. "I have read the books of our fathers. Aquilonia lies beyone the lands of the Stygians and the Shemites, beyond Argos and Zingara; and Cimmeria lies beyond Aquilonia."

"We have each a roving foot," answered Conan carelessly.

"How you won through the forest is a wonder to me," quoth Olmec. "In bygone days a thousand fighting men scarcely were able to carve a road through its perils."

"We encountered a bench-legged monstrosity about the size of a mastodon," said Conan casually, holding out his wine goblet which Techotl filled with evident pleasure. "But when we'd killed it we had no further trouble."

The wine vessel slipped from Techotl's hand to crash on the floor. His dusky skin went ashy. Olmec started to his feet, an image of stunned amazement, and a low gasp of awe or terror breathed up from the others. Some slipped to their knees as if their legs would not support them. Only Tascela seemed not to have heard. Conan glared about him bewilderedly.

"What's the matter? What are you gaping about?"

"You—you slew the dragon-god?"

"God? I killed a dragon. Why not? It was trying to gobble us up."

"But dragons are immortal!" exclaimed Olmec. "They slay each other, but no man ever killed a dragon! The thousand fighting men of our ancestors who fought their way to Xuchotl could not prevail against them! Their swords broke like twigs against their scales!"

"If your ancestors had thought to dip their spears in the poisonous juice of Derketa's Apples," quoth Conan, with his mouth full, "and jab them in the eyes or mouth or somewhere like that, they'd have seen that dragons are no more immortal than any other chunk of beef. The carcass lies at the edge of the trees, just within the forest. If you don't believe me, go and look for yourself."

Olmec shook his head, not in disbelief but in wonder.

"It was because of the dragons that our ancestors took refuge in Xuchotl," said he. "They dared not pass through the plain and plunge into the forest beyond. Scores of them were seized and devoured by the monsters before they could reach the city."

"Then your ancestors didn't build Xuchotl?" asked Valeria.

"It was ancient when they first came into the land. How long it had stood here, not even its degenerate inhabitants knew."

"Your people came from Lake Zuad?" questioned Conan.

"Aye. More than half a century ago a tribe of the Tlazitlans rebelled against the Stygian king, and, being defeated in battle, fled southward. For many weeks they wandered over grasslands, desert and hills, and at last they came into the great forest, a thousand fighting men with their women and children.

"It was in the forest that the dragons fell upon them and tore many to pieces; so the people fled in a frenzy of fear before them, and at last came into the plain and saw the city of Xuchotl in the midst of it.

"They camped before the city, not daring to leave the plain, for the night was made hideous with the noise of the battling monsters through the forest. They made war incessantly upon one another. Yet they came not into the plain.

"The people of the city shut their gates and shot arrows at our people from the walls. The Tlazitlans were imprisoned on the plain, as if the ring of the forest had been a great wall; for to venture into the woods would have been madness.

"That night there came secretly to their camp a slave from the city, one of their own blood, who with a band of exploring soldiers had wandered into the forest long before, when he was a young man. The dragons had devoured all his companions, but he had been taken into the city to dwell in servitude. His name was Tolkemec." A flame lighted the dark eyes at mention of the name, and some of the people muttered obscenely and spat. "He promised to open the gates to the warriors. He asked only that all captives taken be delivered into his hands.

"At dawn he opened the gates. The warriors swarmed in and the halls of Xuchotl ran red. Only a few hundred folk dwelt there, decaying remnants of a once great race. Tolkemec said they came from the east, long ago, from Old Kosala, when the ancestors of those who now dwell in Kosala came up from the south and drove forth the original inhabitants of the land. They wandered far westward and finally found this forest-girdled plain, inhabited then by a tribe of black people.

"These they enslaved and set to building a city. From the hills to the east they brought jade and marble and lapis lazuli, and gold, silver, and copper. Herds of elephants provided them with ivory. When their city was completed, they slew all the black slaves. And their magicians made a terrible magic to guard the city; for by their necromantic arts they re-created the dragons which had once dwelt in this lost land, and whose monstrous bones they found in the forest. Those bones they clothed in flesh and life, and the living beasts walked the earth as they walked it when time was young. But the wizards wove a spell that kept them in the forest and they came not into the plain.

"So for many centuries the people of Xuchotl dwelt in their city, cultivating the fertile plain, until their wise men learned how to grow fruit within the city—fruit which is not planted in soil, but obtains its nourishment out of the air—and then they let the irrigation ditches run dry and dwelt more and more in luxurious sloth, until decay seized them. They were a dying race when our ancestors broke through the forest and came into the plain. Their wizards had died, and the people had forgot their ancient necromancy. They could fight neither by sorcery nor the sword.

"Well, our fathers slew the people of Xuchotl, all except a hundred which were given living into the hands of Tolkemec, who had been their slave; and for many days and nights the halls re-echoed to their screams under the agony of his tortures.

"So the Tlazitlans dwelt here, for a while in peace, ruled by the brothers Tecuhltli and Xotalanc, and by Tolkemec. Tolkemec took a girl of the tribe to wife, and because he had opened the gates, and because he knew many of the arts of the Xuchotlans, he shared the rule of the tribe with the brothers who had led the rebellion and the flight.

"For a few years, then, they dwelt at peace within the city, doing little but eating, drinking, and making love, and raising children. There was no necessity to till the plain, for Tolkemec taught them how to cultivate the air-devouring fruits. Besides, the slaying of the Xuchotlans broke the spell that held the dragons in the forest, and they came nightly and bellowed about the gates of the city. The plain ran red with the blood of their eternal warfare, and it was then that—" He bit his tongue in the midst of the sentence, then presently continued, but Valeria and Conan felt that he had checked an admission he had considered unwise.

"Five years they dwelt in peace. Then"—Olmec's eyes rested briefly on the silent woman at his side—"Xotalanc took a woman to wife, a woman whom both Tecuhltli and old Tolkemec desired. In his madness, Tecuhltli stole her from her husband. Aye, she went willingly enough. Tolkemec, to spite Xotalanc, aided Tecuhltli. Xotalanc demanded that she be given back to him, and the council of the tribe decided that the matter should be left to the woman. She chose to remain with Tecuhltli. In wrath Xotalanc sought to take her back by force, and the retainers of the brothers came to blows in the Great Hall.

"There was much bitterness. Blood was shed on both sides. The quarrel became a feud, the feud an open war. From the welter three factions emerged – Tecuhltli, Xotalanc, and Tolkemec. Already, in the days of peace, they had divided the city between them. Tecuhltli dwelt in the western quarter of the city, Xotalanc in the eastern, and Tolkemec with his family by the southern gate.

"Anger and resentment and jealousy blossomed into bloodshed and rape and murder. Once the sword was drawn there was no turning back; for blood called for blood, and vengeance followed swift on the heels of atrocity. Tecuhltli fought with Xotalanc, and Tolkemec aided first one and then the other, betraying each faction as it fitted his purposes. Tecuhltli and his people withdrew into the quarter of the western gate, where we now sit. Xuchotl is built in the shape of an oval. Tecuhltli, which took its name from its prince, occupies the western end of the oval. The people blocked up all doors connecting the quarter with the rest of the city, except one on each floor, which could be defended easily. They went into the pits below the city and built a wall cutting off the western end of the catacombs, where lie the bodies of the ancient Xuchotlans, and of those Tlazitlans slain in the feud. They dwelt as in a besieged castle, making sorties and forays on their enemies.

"The people of Xotalanc likewise fortified the eastern quarter of the city, and Tolkemec did likewise with the quarter by the southern gate. The central part of the city was left bare and uninhabited. Those empty halls and chambers became a battleground, and a region of brooding terror.

"Tolkemec warred on both clans. He was a fiend in the form of a human, worse than Xotalanc. He knew many secrets of the city he never told the others. From the crypts of the catacombs he plundered the dead of their grisly secrets – secrets of ancient kings and wizards, long forgotten by the degenerate Xuchotlans our ancestors slew. But all his magic did not aid him the night we of Tecuhltli stormed his castle and butchered all his people. Tolkemec we tortured for many days."

His voice sank to a caressing slur, and a faraway look grew in his eyes, as if he looked back over the years to a scene which caused him intense pleasure.

"Aye, we kept the life in him until he screamed for death as for a bride. At last we took him living from the torture chamber and cast him into a dungeon for the rats to gnaw as he died. From that dungeon, somehow, he managed to escape, and dragged himself into the catacombs. There without doubt he died, for the only way out of the catacombs beneath Tecuhltli is through Tecuhltli, and he never emerged by that way. His bones were never found and the superstitious among our people swear that his ghost haunts the crypts to this day, wailing among the bones of the dead. Twelve years ago we butchered the people of Tolkemec, but the feud raged on between Tecuhltli and Xotalanc, as it will rage until the last man, the last woman is dead.

"It was fifty years ago that Tecuhltli stole the wife of Xotalanc. Half a century the feud has endured. I was born in it. All in this chamber, except Tascela, were born in it. We expect to die in it.

"We are a dying race, even as were those Xuchotlans our ancestors slew. When the feud began there were hundreds in each faction. Now we of Tecuhltli number only these you see before you, and the men who guard the four doors: forty in all. How many Xotalancas there are we do not know, but I doubt if they are much more numerous than we. For fifteen years no children have been born to us, and we have seen none among the Xotalancas.

"We are dying, but before we die we will slay as many of the men of Xotalanc as the gods permit."

And with his weird eyes blazing, Olmec spoke long of that grisly feud, fought out in silent chambers and dim halls under the blaze of the green fire-jewels, on floors smoldering with the flames of hell and splashed with deeper crimson from severed veins. In that long butchery a whole generation had perished. Xotalanc was dead, long ago, slain in a grim battle on an ivory stair. Tecuhltli was dead, flayed alive by the maddened Xotalancas who had captured him.

Without emotion Olmec told of hideous battles fought in black corridors, of ambushes on twisting stairs, and red butcheries. With a redder, more abysmal gleam in his deep dark eyes he told of men and women flayed alive, mutilated and dismembered, of captives howling under tortures so ghastly that even the barbarous Cimmerian grunted. No wonder Techotl had trembled with the terror of capture! Yet he had gone forth to slay if he could, driven by hate, that was stronger than his fear. Olmec spoke further, of dark and mysterious matters, of black magic and wizardry conjured out of the black night of the catacombs, of weird creatures invoked out of darkness for horrible allies. In these things the Xotalancas had the advantage, for it was in the eastern catacombs where lay the bones of the greatest wizards of the ancient Xuchotlans, with their immemorial secrets.

Valeria listened with morbid fascination. The feud had become a terrible elemental power driving the people of Xuchotl inexorably on to doom and extinction. It filled their whole lives. They were born in it, and they expected to die in it. They never left their barricaded castle except to steal forth into the Halls of Silence that lay between the opposing fortresses, to slay and be slain. Sometimes the raiders returned with frantic captives, or with grim tokens of victory in fight. Sometimes they did not return at all, or returned only as severed limbs cast down before the bolted bronze doors. It was a ghastly, unreal nightmare existence these people lived, shut off from the rest of the world, caught together like rabid rats in the same trap, butchering one another through the years, crouching and creeping through the sunless corridors to maim and torture and murder.

While Olmec talked, Valeria felt the blazing eyes of Tascela fixed upon her. The princess seemed not to hear what Olmec was saying. Her expression, as he narrated victories or defeats, did not mirror the wild rage or fiendish exultation that alternated on the faces of the other Tecuhltli. The feud that was an obsession to her clansmen seemed meaningless to her. Valeria found her indifferent callousness more repugnant than Olmec's naked ferocity.

"And we can never leave the city," said Olmec. "For fifty years no one has left it except those—" Again he checked himself.

"Even without the peril of the dragons," he continued, "we who were born and raised in the city would not dare leave it. We have never set foot outside the walls. We are not accustomed to the open sky and the naked sun. No; we were born in Xuchotl, and in Xuchotl we shall die."

"Well," said Conan, "with your leave we'll take our chances with the dragons. This feud is none of our business. If you'll show us to the west gate we'll be on our way."

Tascela's hands clenched, and she started to speak, but Olmec interrupted her: "It is nearly nightfall. If you wander forth into the plain by night, you will certainly fall prey to the dragons."

"We crossed it last night, and slept in the open without seeing any," returned Conan.

Tascela smiled mirthlessly. "You dare not leave Xuchotl!"

Conan glared at her with instinctive antagonism; she was not looking at him, but at the woman opposite him.

"I think they dare," stated Olmec. "But look you, Conan and Valeria, the gods must have sent you to us, to cast victory into the laps of the Tecuhltli! You are professional fighters—why not fight for us? We have wealth in abundance—precious jewels are as common in Xuchotl as cobblestones are in the cities of the world. Some the Xuchotlans brought with them from Kosala. Some, like the firestones, they found in the hills to the east. Aid us to wipe out the Xotalancas, and we will give you all the jewels you can carry."

"And will you help us destroy the dragons?" asked Valeria. "With bows and poisoned arrows thirty men could slay all the dragons in the forest."

"Aye!" replied Olmec promptly. "We have forgotten the use of the bow, in years of hand-to-hand fighting, but we can learn again."

"What do you say?" Valeria inquired of Conan.

"We're both penniless vagabonds," he grinned hardily. "I'd as soon kill Xotalancas as anybody."

"Then you agree?" exclaimed Olmec, while Techotl fairly hugged himself with delight.

"Aye. And now suppose you show us chambers where we can sleep, so we can be fresh tomorrow for the beginning of the slaying."

Olmec nodded, and waved a hand, and Techotl and a woman led the adventurers into a corridor which led through a door off to the left of the jade dais. A glance back showed Valeria Olmec sitting on his throne, chin on knotted fist, staring after them. His eyes burned with a weird flame. Tascela leaned back in her seat, whispering to the sullen-faced maid, Yasala, who leaned over her shoulder, her ear to the princess's moving lips.

The hallway was not so broad as most they had traversed, but it was long. Presently the woman halted, opened a door, and drew aside for Valeria to enter.

"Wait a minute," growled Conan. "Where do I sleep?"

Techotl pointed to a chamber across the hallway, but one door farther down. Conan hesitated, and seemed inclined to raise an objection, but Valeria smiled spitefully at him and shut the door in his face. He muttered something uncomplimentary about women in general, and strode off down the corridor after Techotl.

In the ornate chamber where he was to sleep, he glanced up at the slot- like skylights. Some were wide enough to admit the body of a slender man, supposing the glass were broken.

"Why don't the Xotalancas come over the roofs and shatter those skylights?" he asked.

"They cannot be broken," answered Techotl. "Besides, the roofs would be hard to clamber over. They are mostly spires and domes and steep ridges."

He volunteered more information about the "castle" of Tecuhltli. Like the rest of the city it contained four stories, or tiers of chambers, with towers jutting up from the roof. Each tier was named; indeed, the people of Xuchotl had a name for each chamber, hall, and stair in the city, as people of more normal cities designate streets and quarters. In Tecuhltli the floors were named The Eagle's Tier, The Ape's Tier, The Tiger's Tier and The Serpent's Tier, in the order as enumerated, The Eagle's Tier being the highest, or fourth, floor.

"Who is Tascela?" asked Conan. "Olmec's wife?"

Techotl shuddered and glanced furtively about him before answering.

"No. She is—Tascela! She was the wife of Xotalanc—the woman Tecuhltli stole, to start the feud."

"What are you talking about?" demanded Conan. "That woman is beautiful and young. Are you trying to tell me that she was a wife fifty years ago?"

"Aye! I swear it! She was a full-grown woman when the Tlazitlans journeyed from Lake Zuad. It was because the king of Stygia desired her for a concubine that Xotalanc and his brother rebelled and fled into the wilderness. She is a witch, who possesses the secret of perpetual youth."

"What's that?" asked Conan.

Techotl shuddered again.

"Ask me not! I dare not speak. It is too grisly, even for Xuchotl!"

And touching his finger to his lips, he glided from the chamber.

4. — SCENT OF BLACK LOTUS

VALERIA unbuckled her sword belt and laid it with the sheathed weapon on the couch where she meant to sleep. She noted that the doors were supplied with bolts, and asked where they led.

"Those lead to adjoining chambers," answered the woman, indicating the doors on right and left. "That one"—pointing to a copper-bound door opposite that which opened into the corridor—"leads to a corridor which runs to a stair that descends into the catacombs. Do not fear; naught can harm you here."

"Who spoke of fear?" snapped Valeria. "I just like to know what sort of harbor I'm dropping anchor in. No, I don't want you to sleep at the foot of my couch. I'm not accustomed to being waited on—not by women, anyway. You have my leave to go."

Alone in the room, the pirate shot the bolts on all the doors, kicked off her boots and stretched luxuriously out on the couch. She imagined Conan similarly situated across the corridor, but her feminine vanity prompted her to visualize him as scowling and muttering with chagrin as he cast himself on his solitary couch, and she grinned with gleeful malice as she prepared herself for slumber.

Outside, night had fallen. In the halls of Xuchotl the green fire-jewels blazed like the eyes of prehistoric cats. Somewhere among the dark towers, a night wind moaned like a restless spirit. Through the dim passages, stealthy figures began stealing, like disembodied shadows.

Valeria awoke suddenly on her couch. In the dusky emerald glow of the fire-gems she saw a shadowy figure bending over her. For a bemused instant the apparition seemed part of the dream she had been dreaming. She had seemed to lie on the couch in the chamber as she was actually lying, while over her pulsed and throbbed a gigantic black blossom so enormous that it hid the ceiling. Its exotic perfume pervaded her being, inducing a delicious, sensuous languor that was something more and less than sleep. She was sinking into scented billows of insensible bliss, when something touched her face. So supersensitive were her drugged senses, that the light touch was like a dislocating impact, jolting her rudely into full wakefulness. Then it was that she saw, not a gargantuan blossom, but a dark-skinned woman standing above her.

With the realization came anger and instant action. The woman turned lithely, but before she could run Valeria was on her feet and had caught her arm. She fought like a wildcat for an instant, and then subsided as she felt herself crushed by the superior strength of her captor. The pirate wrenched the woman around to face her, caught her chin with her free hand and forced her captive to meet her gaze. It was the sullen Yasala, Tascela's maid.

"What the devil were you doing bending over me? What's that in your hand?"

The woman made no reply, but sought to cast away the object. Valeria twisted her arm around in front of her, and the thing fell to the floor – a great black exotic blossom on a jade-green stem, large as a woman's head, to be sure, but tiny beside the exaggerated vision she had seen.

"The black lotus!" said Valeria between her teeth. "The blossom whose scent brings deep sleep. You were trying to drug me! If you hadn't accidentally touched my face with the petals, you'd have—why did you do it? What's your game?"

Yasala maintained a sulky silence, and with an oath Valeria whirled her around, forced her to her knees and twisted her arm up behind her back.

"Tell me, or I'll tear your arm out of its socket!"

Yasala squirmed in anguish as her arm was forced excruciatingly up between her shoulder blades, but a violent shaking of her head was the only answer she made.

"Slut!" Valeria cast her from her to sprawl on the floor. The pirate glared at the prostrate figure with blazing eyes. Fear and the memory of Tascela's burning eyes stirred in her, rousing all her tigerish instincts of self-preservation. These people were decadent; any sort of perversity might be expected to be encountered among them. But Valeria sensed here something that moved behind the scenes, some secret terror fouler than common degeneracy. Fear and revulsion of this weird city swept her. These people were neither sane nor normal; she began to doubt if they were even human. Madness smoldered in the eyes of them all—all except the cruel, cryptic eyes of Tascela, which held secrets and mysteries more abysmal than madness.

She lifted her head and listened intently. The halls of Xuchotl were as silent as if it were in reality a dead city. The green jewels bathed the chamber in a nightmare glow, in which the eyes of the woman on the floor glittered eerily up at her. A thrill of panic throbbed through Valeria, driving the last vestige of mercy from her fierce soul.

"Why did you try to drug me?" she muttered, grasping the woman's black hair, and forcing her head back to glare into her sullen, long-lashed eyes. "Did Tascela send you?"

No answer. Valeria cursed venomously and slapped the woman first on one cheek and then the other. The blows resounded through the room, but Yasala made no outcry.

"Why don't you scream?" demanded Valeria savagely. "Do you fear someone will hear you? Whom do you fear? Tascela? Olmec? Conan?"

Yasala made no reply. She crouched, watching her captor with eyes baleful as those of a basilisk. Stubborn silence always fans anger. Valeria turned and tore a handful of cords from a near-by hanging.

"You sulky slut!" she said between her teeth. "I'm going to strip you stark naked and tie you across that couch and whip you until you tell me what you were doing here, and who sent you!"

Yasala made no verbal protest, nor did she offer any resistance, as Valeria carried out the first part of her threat with a fury that her captive's obstinacy only sharpened. Then for a space there was no sound in the chamber except the whistle and crackle of hard-woven silken cords on naked flesh. Yasala could not move her fast-bound hands or feet. Her body writhed and quivered under the chastisement, her head swayed from side to side in rhythm with the blows. Her teeth were sunk into her lower lip and a trickle of blood began as the punishment continued. But she did not cry out.

The pliant cords made no great sound as they encountered the quivering body of the captive; only a sharp crackling snap, but each cord left a red streak across Yasala's dark flesh. Valeria inflicted the punishment with all the strength of her war-hardened arm, with all the mercilessness acquired during a life where pain and torment were daily happenings, and with all the cynical ingenuity which only a woman displays toward a woman.

Yasala suffered more, physically and mentally, than she would have suffered under a lash wielded by a man, however strong.

It was the application of this feminine cynicism which at last tamed Yasala.

A low whimper escaped from her lips, and Valeria paused, arm lifted, and raked back a damp yellow lock. "Well, are you going to talk?" she demanded. "I can keep this up all night, if necessary."

"Mercy!" whispered the woman. "I will tell."

Valeria cut the cords from her wrists and ankles, and pulled her to her feet. Yasala sank down on the couch, half reclining on one bare hip, supporting herself on her arm, and writhing at the contact of her smarting flesh with the couch. She was trembling in every limb.

"Wine!" she begged, dry-lipped, indicating with a quivering hand a gold vessel on an ivory table. "Let me drink. I am weak with pain. Then I will tell you all."

Valeria picked up the vessel, and Yasala rose unsteadily to receive it. She took it, raised it toward her lips—then dashed the contents full into the Aquilonian's face. Valeria reeled backward, shaking and clawing the stinging liquid out of her eyes. Through a smarting mist she saw Yasala dart across the room, fling back a bolt, throw open the copper-bound door and run down the hall. The pirate was after her instantly, sword out and murder in her heart.

But Yasala had the start, and she ran with the nervous agility of a woman who has just been whipped to the point of hysterical frenzy. She rounded a corner in the corridor, yards ahead of Valeria, and when the pirate turned it, she saw only an empty hall, and at the other end a door that gaped blackly. A damp moldy scent reeked up from it, and Valeria shivered. That must be the door that led to the catacombs. Yasala had taken refuge among the dead.

Valeria advanced to the door and looked down a flight of stone steps that vanished quickly into utter blackness. Evidently it was a shaft that led straight to the pits below the city, without opening upon any of the lower floors. She shivered slightly at the thought of the thousands of corpses lying in their stone crypts down there, wrapped in their moldering cloths. She had no intention of groping her way down those stone steps. Yasala doubtless knew every turn and twist of the subterranean tunnels.

She was turning back, baffled and furious, when a sobbing cry welled up from the blackness. It seemed to come from a great depth, but human words were faintly distinguishable, and the voice was that of a woman. "Oh, help! Help, in Set's name! Ahhh!" It trailed away, and Valeria thought she caught the echo of a ghostly tittering.

Valeria felt her skin crawl. What had happened to Yasala down there in the thick blackness? There was no doubt that it had been she who had cried out. But what peril could have befallen her? Was a Xotalanca lurking down there? Olmec had assured them that the catacombs below Tecuhltli were walled off from the rest, too securely for their enemies to break through. Besides, that tittering had not sounded like a human being at all.

Valeria hurried back down the corridor, not stopping to close the door that opened on the stair. Regaining her chamber, she closed the door and shot the bolt behind her. She pulled on her boots and buckled her sword-belt about her. She was determined to make her way to Conan's room and urge him, if he still lived, to join her in an attempt to fight their way out of that city of devils.

But even as she reached the door that opened into the corridor, a long- drawn scream of agony rang through the halls, followed by the stamp of running feet and the loud clangor of swords.

5. — TWENTY RED NAILS

TWO WARRIORS lounged in the guardroom on the floor known as the Tier of the Eagle. Their attitude was casual, though habitually alert. An attack on the great bronze door from without was always a possibility, but for many years no such assault had been attempted on either side.

"The strangers are strong allies," said one. "Olmec will move against the enemy tomorrow, I believe."

He spoke as a soldier in a war might have spoken. In the miniature world of Xuchotl each handful of feudists was an army, and the empty halls between the castles was the country over which they campaigned.

The other meditated for a space.

"Suppose with their aid we destroy Xotalanc," he said. "What then, Xatmec?"

"Why," returned Xatmec, "we will drive red nails for them all. The captives we will burn and flay and quarter."

"But afterward?" pursued the other. "After we have slain them all? Will it not seem strange to have no foe to fight? All my life I have fought and hated the Xotalancas. With the feud ended, what is left?"

Xatmec shrugged his shoulders. His thoughts had never gone beyond the destruction of their foes. They could not go beyond that.

Suddenly both men stiffened at a noise outside the door.

"To the door, Xatmec!" hissed the last speaker. "I shall look through the Eye—"

Xatmec, sword in hand, leaned against the bronze door, straining his ear to hear through the metal. His mate looked into the mirror. He started convulsively. Men were clustered thickly outside the door; grim, dark-faced men with swords gripped in their teeth—and their fingers thrust into their ears. One who wore a feathered headdress had a set of pipes whch he set to his lips, and even as the Tecuhltli started to shout a warning, the pipes began to skirl.

The cry died in the guard's throat as the thin, weird piping penetrated the metal door and smote on his ears. Xatmec leaned frozen against the door, as if paralyzed in that position. His face was that of a wooden image, his expression one of horrified listening. The other guard, farther removed from the source of the sound, yet sensed the horror of what was taking place, the grisly threat that lay in that demoniac fifing. He felt the weird strains plucking like unseen fingers at the tissues of his brain, filling him with alien emotions and impulses of madness. But with a soul-tearing effort he broke the spell, and shrieked a warning in a voice he did not recognize as his own.

But even as he cried out, the music changed to an unbearable shrilling that was like a knife in the eardrums. Xatmec screamed in sudden agony, and all the sanity went out of his face like a flame blown out in a wind. Like a madman he ripped loose the chain, tore open the door and rushed out into the hall, sword lifted before his mate could stop him. A dozen blades struck him down, and over his mangled body the Xotalancas surged into the guardroom, with a long-drawn, blood-mad yell that sent the unwonted echoes reverberating.

His brain reeling from the shock of it all, the remaining guard leaped to meet them with goring spear. The horror of the sorcery he had just witnessed was submerged in the stunning realization that the enemy were in Tecuhltli. And as his spearhead ripped through a dark-skinned belly he knew no more, for a swinging sword crushed his skull, even as wild-eyed warriors came pouring in from the chambers behind the guardroom.

It was the yelling of men and the clanging of steel that brought Conan bounding from his couch, wide awake and broadsword in hand. In an instant he had reached the door and flung it open, and was glaring out into the corridor just as Techotl rushed up it, eyes blazing madly.

"The Xotalancas!" he screamed, in a voice hardly human. "They are within the door!"

Conan ran down the corridor, even as Valeria emerged from her chamber.

"What the devil is it?" she called.

"Techotl says the Xotalancas are in," he answered hurriedly. "That racket sounds like it."

With the Tecuhltli on their heels they burst into the throne room and were confronted by a scene beyond the most frantic dream of blood and fury. Twenty men and women, their black hair streaming, and the white skulls gleaming on their breasts, were locked in combat with the people of Tecuhltli. The women on both sides fought as madly as the men, and already the room and the hall beyond were strewn with corpses.

Olmec, naked but for a breech-clout, was fighting before his throne, and as the adventurers entered, Tascela ran from an inner chamber with a sword in her hand.

Xatmec and his mate were dead, so there was none to tell the Tecuhltli how their foes had found their way into their citadel. Nor was there any to say what had prompted that mad attempt. But the losses of the Xotalancas had been greater, their position more desperate, than the Tecuhltli had known. The maiming of their scaly ally, the destruction of the Burning Skull, and the news, gasped by a dying man, that mysterious white-skin allies had joined their enemies, had driven them to the frenzy of desperation and the wild determination to die dealing death to their ancient foes.

The Tecuhltli, recovering from the first stunning shock of the surprise that had swept them back into the throne room and littered the floor with their corpses, fought back with an equally desperate fury, while the doorguards from the lower floors came racing to hurl themselves into the fray. It was the death fight of rabid wolves, blind, panting, merciless. Back and forth it surged, from door to dais, blades whickering and striking into flesh, blood spurting, feet stamping the crimson floor where redder pools were forming. Ivory tables crashed over, seats were splintered, velvet hangings torn down were stained red. It was the bloody climax of a bloody half-century, and every man there sensed it.

But the conclusion was inevitable. The Tecuhltli outnumbered the invaders almost two to one, and they were heartened by that fact and by the entrance into the melee of their light-skinned allies.

These crashed into the fray with the devastating effect of a hurricane plowing through a grove of saplings. In sheer strength no three Tlazitlans were a match for Conan, and in spite of his weight he was quicker on his feet than any of them. He moved through the whirling, eddying mass with the surety and destructiveness of a gray wolf amidst a pack of alley curs, and he strode over a wake of crumpled figures.

Valeria fought beside him, her lips smiling and her eyes blazing. She was stronger than the average man, and far quicker and more ferocious. Her sword was like a living thing in her hand. Where Conan beat down opposition by the sheer weight and power of his blows, breaking spears, splitting skulls and cleaving bosoms to the breastbone, Valeria brought into action a finesse of swordplay that dazzled and bewildered her antagonists before it slew them. Again and again a warrior, heaving high his heavy blade, found her point in his jugular before he could strike. Conan, towering above the field, strode through the welter smiting right and left, but Valeria moved like an illusive phantom, constantly shifting, and thrusting and slashing as she shifted. Swords missed her again and again as the wielders flailed the empty air and died with her point in their hearts or throats, and her mocking laughter in their ears.

Neither sex nor condition was considered by the maddened combatants. The five women of the Xotalancas were down with thir throats cut before Conan and Valeria entered the fray, and when a man or woman went down under the stamping feet, there was always a knife ready for the helpless throat, or a sandaled foot eager to crush the prostrate skull.

From wall to wall, from door to door rolled the waves of combat, spilling over into adjoining chambers. And presently only Tecuhltli and their white-skinned allies stood upright in the great throne room. The survivors stared bleakly and blankly at each other, like survivors after Judgement Day or the destruction of the world. On legs wide-braced, hands gripping notched and dripping swords, blood trickling down their arms, they stared at one another across the mangled corpses of friends and foes. They had no breath left to shout, but a bestial mad howling rose from their lips. It was not a human cry of triumph. It was the howling of a rabid wolf-pack stalking among the bodies of its victims.

Conan caught Valeria's arm and turned her about.

"You've got a stab in the calf of your leg," he growled.

She glanced down, for the first time aware of a stinging in the muscles of her leg. Some dying man on the floor had fleshed his dagger with his last effort.

"You look like a butcher yourself," she laughed.

He shook a red shower from his hands.

"Not mine. Oh, a scratch here and there. Nothing to bother about. But that calf ought to be bandaged."

Olmec came through the litter, looking like a ghoul with his naked massive shoulders splashed with blood, and his black beard dabbled in crimson. His eyes were red, like the reflection of flame on black water.

"We have won!" he croaked dazedly. "The feud is ended! The dogs of Xotalanc lie dead! Oh, for a captive to flay alive! Yet it is good to look upon their dead faces. Twenty dead dogs! Twenty red nails for the black column!"

"You'd best see to your wounded," grunted Conan, turning away from him. "Here, girl, let me see that leg."

"Wait a minute!" she shook him off impatiently. The fire of fighting still burned brightly in her soul. "How do we know these are all of them? These might have come on a raid of their own."

"They would not split the clan on a foray like this," said Olmec, shaking his head, and regaining some of his ordinary intelligence. Without his purple robe the man seemed less like a prince than some repellent beast of prey. "I will stake my head upon it that we have slain them all. There were less of them than I dreamed, and they must have been desperate. But how came they in Tecuhltli?"

Tascela came forward, wiping her sword on her naked thigh, and holding in her other hand an object she had taken from the body of the feathered leader of the Xotalancas.

"The pipes of madness," she said. "A warrior tells me that Xatmec opened the door to the Xotalancas and was cut down as they stormed into the guardroom. This warrior came to the guardroom from the inner hall just in time to see it happen and to hear the last of a weird strain of music which froze his very soul. Tolkemec used to talk of these pipes, which the Xuchotlans swore were hidden somewhere in the catacombs with the bones of the ancient wizard who used them in his lifetime. Somehow the dogs of Xotalanc found them and learned their secret."

"Somebody ought to go to Xotalanc and see if any remain alive," said Conan. "I'll go if somebody will guide me."

Olmec glanced at the remnants of his people. There were only twenty left alive, and of these several lay groaning on the floor. Tascela was the only one of the Tecuhltli who had escaped without a wound. The princess was untouched, though she had fought as savagely as any.

"Who will go with Conan to Xotalanc?" asked Olmec.

Techotl limped forward. The wound in his thigh had started bleeding afresh, and he had another gash across his ribs.

"I will go!"

"No, you won't," vetoed Conan. "And you're not going either, Valeria. In a little while that leg will be getting stiff."

"I will go," volunteered a warrior, who was knotting a bandage about a slashed forearm.

"Very well, Yanath. Go with the Cimmerian. And you, too, Topal." Olmec indicated another man whose injuries were slight. "But first aid to lift the badly wounded on these couches where we may bandage their hurts."

This was done quickly. As they stooped to pick up a woman who had been stunned by a warclub, Olmec's beard brushed Topal's ear. Conan thought the prince muttered something to the warrior, but he could not be sure. A few moments later he was leading his companions down the hall.

Conan glanced back as he went out the door, at that shambles where the dead lay on the smoldering floor, blood-stained dark limbs knotted in attitudes of fierce muscular effort, dark faces frozen in masks of hate, glassy eyes glaring up at the green fire-jewels which bathed the ghastly scene in a dusky emerald witchlight. Among the dead the living moved aimlessly, like people moving in a trance. Conan heard Olmec call a woman and direct her to bandage Valeria's leg. The pirate followed the woman into an adjoining chamber, already beginning to limp slightly.

Warily the two Tecuhltli led Conan along the hall beyond the bronze door, and through chamber after chamber shimmering in the green fire. They saw no one, heard no sound. After they crossed the Great Hall which bisected the city from north to south, their caution was increased by the realization of their nearness to enemy territory. But chambers and halls lay empty to their wary gaze, and they came at last along a broad dim hallway and halted before a bronze door similar to the Eagle Door of Tecuhltli. Gingerly they tried it, and it opened silently under their fingers. Awed, they stared into the green-lit chambers beyond. For fifty years no Tecuhltli had entered those halls save as a prisoner going to a hideous doom. To go to Xotalanc had been the ultimate horror that could befall a man of the western castle. The terror of it had stalked through their dreams since earliest childhood. To Yanath and Topol that bronze door was like the portal of hell.

They cringed back, unreasoning horror in their eyes, and Conan pushed past them and strode into Xotalanc.

Timidly they followed him. As each man set foot over the threshold he stared and glared wildly about him. But only their quick, hurried breathing disturbed the silence.

They had come into a square guardroom, like that behind the Eagle Door of Tecuhltli, and, similarly, a hall ran away from it to a broad chamber that was a counterpart of Olmec's throne room.

Conan glanced down the hall with its rugs and divans and hangings, and stood listening intently. He heard no noise, and the rooms had an empty feel. He did not believe there were any Xotalancas left alive in Xuchotl.

"Come on," he muttered, and started down the hall.

He had not gone far when he was aware that only Yanath was following him. He wheeled back to see Topol standing in an attitude of horror, one arm out as if to fend off some threatening peril, his distended eyes fixed with hypnotic intensity on something protruding from behind a divan.

"What the devil?" Then Conan saw what Topol was staring at, and he felt a faint twitching of the skin between his giant shoulders. A monstrous head protruded from behind the divan, a reptilian head, broad as the head of a crocodile, with down-curving fangs that projected over the lower jaw. But there was an unnatural limpness about the thing, and the hideous eyes were glazed.

Conan peered behind the couch. It was a great serpent which lay there limp in death, but such a serpent as he had never seen in his wanderings. The reek and chill of the deep black earth were about it, and its color was an indeterminable hue which changed with each new angle from which he surveyed it. A great wound in the neck showed what had caused its death.

"It is the Crawler!" whispered Yanath.

"It's the thing I slashed on the stair," grunted Conan. "After it trailed us to the Eagle Door, it dragged itself here to die. How could the Xotalancas control such a brute?"

The Tecuhltli shivered and shook their heads.

"They brought it up from the black tunnels below the catacombs. They discovered secrets unknown to Tecuhltli."

"Well, it's dead, and if they'd had any more of them, they'd have brought them along when they came to Tecuhltli. Come on."

They crowded close at his heels as he strode down the hall and thrust on the silver-worked door at the other end.

"If we don't find anybody on this floor," he said, "we'll descend into the lower floors. We'll explore Xotalanc from the roof to the catacombs. If Xotalanc is like Tecuhltli, all the rooms and halls in this tier will be lighted—what the devil!"

They had come into the broad throne chamber, so similar to that one in Tecuhltli. There were the same jade dais and ivory seat, the same divans, rugs and hangings on the walls. No black, red-scarred column stood behind the throne-dais, but evidences of the grim feud were not lacking.

Ranged along the wall behind the dais were rows of glass-covered shelves. And on those shelves hundreds of human heads, perfectly preserved, stared at the startled watchers with emotionless eyes, as they had stared for only the gods knew how many months and years.

Topal muttered a curse, but Yanath stood silent, the mad light growing in his wide eyes. Conan frowned, knowing that Tlazitlan sanity was hung on a hair-trigger.

Suddenly Yanath pointed to the ghastly relics with a twitching finger.

"There is my brother's head!" he murmured. "And there is my father's younger brother! And there beyond them is my sister's eldest son!"

Suddenly he began to weep, dry-eyed, with harsh, loud sobs that shook his frame. He did not take his eyes from the heads. His sobs grew shriller, changed to frightful, high-pitched laughter, and that in turn became an unbearable screaming. Yanath was stark mad.

Conan laid a hand on his shoulder, and as if the touch had released all the frenzy in his soul, Yanath screamed and whirled, striking at the Cimmerian with his sword. Conan parried the blow, and Topal tried to catch Yanath's arm. But the madman avoided him and with froth flying from his lips, he drove his sword deep into Topal's body. Topal sank down with a groan, and Yanath whirled for an instant like a crazy dervish; then he ran at the shelves and began hacking at the glass with his sword, screeching blasphemously.

Conan sprang at him from behind, trying to catch him unaware and disarm him, but the madman wheeled and lunged at him, screaming like a lost soul. Realizing that the warrior was hopelessly insane, the Cimmerian side-stepped, and as the maniac went past, he swung a cut that severed the shoulder-bone and breast, and dropped the man dead beside his dying victim.

Conan bent over Topal, seeing that the man was at his last gasp. It was useless to seek to stanch the blood gushing from the horrible wound.

"You're done for, Topal," grunted Conan. "Any word you want to send to your people?"

"Bend closer," gasped Topal, and Conan complied—and an instant later caught the man's wrist as Topal struck at his breast with a dagger.

"Crom!" swore Conan. "Are you mad, too?"

"Olmec ordered it!" gasped the dying man. "I know not why. As we lifted the wounded upon the couches he whispered to me, bidding me to slay you as we returned to Tecuhltli—" And with the name of his clan on his lips, Topal died.

Conan scowled down at him in puzzlement. This whole affair had an aspect of lunacy. Was Olmec mad, too? Were all the Tecuhltli madder than he had realized? With a shrug of his shoulders he strode down the hall and out of the bronze door, leaving the dead Tecuhltli lying before the staring dead eyes of their kinsmen's heads.

Conan needed no guide back through the labryinth they had traversed. His primitive instinct of direction led him unerringly along the route they had come. He traversed it as warily as he had before, his sword in his hand, and his eyes fiercely searching each shadowed nook and corner; for it was his former allies he feared now, not the ghosts of the slain Xotalancas.

He had crossed the Great Hall and entered the chambers beyond when he heard something moving ahead of him—something which gasped and panted, and moved with a strange, floundering, scrambling noise. A moment later Conan saw a man crawling over the flaming floor toward him—a man whose progress left a broad bloody smear on the smoldering surface. It was Techotl and his eyes were already glazing; from a deep gash in his breast blood gushed steadily between the fingers of his clutching hand. With the other he clawed and hitched himself along.

"Conan," he cried chokingly, "Conan! Olmec has taken the yellow-haired woman!"

"So that's why he told Topal to kill me!" murmured Conan, dropping to his knee beside the man, who his experienced eye told him was dying. "Olmec isn't as mad as I thought."

Techotl's groping fingers plucked at Conan's arm. In the cold, loveless, and altogether hideous life of the Tecuhltli, his admiration and affection for the invaders from the outer world formed a warm, human oasis, constituted a tie that connected him with a more natural humanity that was totally lacking in his fellows, whose only emotions were hate, lust, and the urge of sadistic cruelty.

"I sought to oppose him," gurgled Techotl, blood bubbling frothily to his lips. "But he struck me down. He thought he had slain me, but I crawled away. Ah, Set, how far I have crawled in my own blood! Beware, Conan! Olmec may have set an ambush for your return! Slay Olmec! He is a beast. Take Valeria and flee! Fear not to traverse the forest. Olmec and Tascela lied about the dragons. They slew each other years ago, all save the strongest. For a dozen years there has been only one dragon. If you have slain him, there is naught in the forest to harm you. He was the god Olmec worshipped; and Olmec fed human sacrifices to him, the very old and the very young, bound and hurled from the wall. Hasten! Olmec has taken Valeria to the Chamber of the—"

His head slumped down and he was dead before it came to rest on the floor.

Conan sprang up, his eyes like live coals. So that was Olmec's game, having first used the strangers to destroy his foes! He should have known that something of the sort would be going on in that black-bearded degenerate's mind.

The Cimmerian started toward Tecuhltli with reckless speed. Rapidly he reckoned the numbers of his former allies. Only twenty-one, counting Olmec, had survived that fiendish battle in the throne room. Three had died since, which left seventeen enemies with which to reckon. In his rage Conan felt capable of accounting for the whole clan single-handed.

But the innate craft of the wilderness rose to guide his berserk rage. He remembered Techotl's warning of an ambush. It was quite probable that the prince would make such provisions, on the chance that Topal might have failed to carry out his order. Olmec would be expecting him to return by the same route he had followed in going to Xotalanc.

Conan glanced up at a skylight under which he was passing and caught the blurred glimmer of stars. They had not yet begun to pale for dawn. The events of the night had been crowded into a comparatively short space of time.

He turned aside from his direct course and descended a winding staircase to the floor below. He did not know where the door was to be found that let into the castle on that level, but he knew he could find it. How he was to force the locks he did not know; he believed that the doors of Tecuhltli would all be locked and bolted, if for no other reason than the habits of half a century. But there was nothing else but to attempt it.

Sword in hand, he hurried noiselessly on through a maze of green-lit or shadowy rooms and halls. He knew he must be near Tecuhltli, when a sound brought him up short. He recognized it for what it was—a human being trying to cry out through a stifling gag. It came from somewhere ahead of him, and to the left. In those deathly-still chambers a small sound carried a long way.

Conan turned aside and went seeking after the sound, which continued to be repeated. Presently he was glaring through a doorway upon a weird scene. In the room into which he was looking a low rack-like frame of iron lay on the floor, and a giant figure was bound prostrate upon it. His head rested on a bed of iron spikes, which were already crimson-pointed with blood where they had pierced his scalp. A peculiar harness-like contrivance was fastened about his head, though in such a manner that the leather band did not protect his scalp from the spikes. This harness was connected by a slender chain to the mechanism that upheld a huge iron ball which was suspended above the captive's hairy breast. As long as the man could force himself to remain motionless the iron ball hung in its place. But when the pain of the iron points caused him to lift his head, the ball lurched downward a few inches. Presently his aching neck muscles would no longer support his head in its unnatural position and it would fall back on the spikes again. It was obvious that eventually the ball would crush him to a pulp, slowly and inexorably. The victim was gagged, and above the gag his great black ox-eyes rolled wildly toward the man in the doorway, who stood in silent amazement. The man on the rack was Olmec, prince of Tecuhltli.

6. — THE EYES OF TASCELA

"WHY did you bring me into this chamber to bandage my leg?" demanded Valeria. "Couldn't you have done it just as well in the throne room?"

She sat on a couch with her wounded leg extended upon it, and the Tecuhltli woman had just bound it with silk bandages. Valeria's red-stained sword lay on the couch beside her.

She frowned as she spoke. The woman had done her task silently and efficiently, but Valeria liked neither the lingering, caressing touch of her slim fingers nor the expression in her eyes.

"They have taken the rest of the wounded into the other chambers," answered the woman in the soft speech of the Tecuhltli women, which somehow did not suggest either softness or gentleness in the speakers. A little while before, Valeria had seen this same woman stab a Xotalanca woman through the breast and stamp the eyeballs out of a wounded Xotalanca man.

"They will be carrying the corpses of the dead down into the catacombs," she added, "lest the ghosts escape into the chambers and dwell there."

"Do you believe in ghosts?" asked Valeria.

"I know the ghost of Tolkemec dwells in the catacombs," she answered with a shiver. "Once I saw it, as I crouched in a crypt among the bones of a dead queen. It passed by in the form of an ancient man with flowing white beard and locks, and luminous eyes that blazed in the darkness. It was Tolkemec; I saw him living when I was a child and he was being tortured."

Her voice sank to a fearful whisper: "Olmec laughs, but I know Tolkemec's ghost dwells in the catacombs! They say it is rats whch gnaw the flesh from the bones of the newly dead—but ghosts eat flesh. Who knows but that—"

She glanced up quickly as a shadow fell across the couch. Valeria looked up to see Olmec gazing down at her. The prince had cleansed his hands, torso, and beard of the blood that had splashed them; but he had not donned his robe, and his great dark-skinned hairless body and limbs renewed the impression of strength bestial in its nature. His deep black eyes burned with a more elemental light, and there was the suggestion of a twitching in the fingers that tugged at his thick blue-black beard.

He stared fixedly at the woman, and she rose and glided from the chamber. As she passed through the door she cast a look over her shoulder at Valeria, a glance full of cynical derision and obscene mockery.

"She has done a clumsy job," criticized the prince, coming to the divan and bending over the bandage. "Let me see—"

With a quickness amazing in one of his bulk he snatched her sword and threw it across the chamber. His next move was to catch her in his giant arms.

Quick and unexpected as the move was, she almost matched it; for even as he grabbed her, her dirk was in her hand and she stabbed murderously at his throat. More by luck than skill he caught her wrist, and then began a savage wrestling-match. She fought him with fists, feet, knees, teeth, and nails, with all the strength of her magnificent body and all the knowledge of hand-to-hand fighting she had acquired in her years of roving and fighting on sea and land. It availed her nothing against his brute strength. She lost her dirk in the first moment of contact, and thereafter found herself powerless to inflict any appreciable pain on her giant attacker.

The blaze in his weird black eyes did not alter, and their expression filled her with fury, fanned by the sardonic smile that seemed carved upon his bearded lips. Those eyes and that smile contained all the cruel cynicism that seethes below the surface of a sophisticated and degenerate race, and for the first time in her life Valeria experienced fear of a man. It was like struggling against some huge elemental force; his iron arms thwarted her efforts with an ease that sent panic racing through her limbs. He seemed impervious to any pain she could inflict. Only once, when she sank her white teeth savagely into his wrist so that the blood started, did he react. And that was to buffet her brutally upon the side of the head with his open hand, so that stars flashed before her eyes and her head rolled on her shoulders.

Her shirt had been torn open in the struggle, and with cynical cruelty he rasped his thick beard across her bare breasts, bringing the blood to suffuse the fair skin, and fetching a cry of pain and outraged fury from her. Her convulsive resistance was useless; she was crushed down on a couch, disarmed and panting, her eyes blazing up at him like the eyes of a trapped tigress.

A moment later he was hurrying from the chamber, carrying her in his arms. She made no resistance, but the smoldering of her eyes showed that she was unconquered in spirit, at least. She had not cried out. She knew that Conan was not within call, and it did not occur to her that any in Tecuhltli would oppose their prince. But she noticed that Olmec went stealthily, with his head on one side as if listening for sounds of pursuit, and he did not return to the throne chamber. He carried her through a door that stood opposite that through which he had entered, crossed another room and began stealing down a hall. As she became convinced that he feared some opposition to the abduction, she threw back her head and screamed at the top of her lusty voice.

She was rewarded by a slap that half-stunned her, and Olmec quickened his pace to a shambling run.

But her cry had been echoed and, twisting her head about, Valeria, through the tears and stars that partly blinded her, saw Techotl limping after them.

Olmec turned with a snarl, shifting the woman to an uncomfortable and certainly undignified position under one huge arm, where he held her writhing and kicking vainly, like a child.

"Olmec!" protested Techotl. "You cannot be such a dog as to do this thing! She is Conan's woman! She helped us slay the Xotalancas, and—"

Without a word Olmec balled his free hand into a huge fist and stretched the wounded warrior senseless at his feet. Stooping, and hindered not at all by the struggles and imprecations of his captive, he drew Techotl's sword from its sheath and stabbed the warrior in the breast. Then casting aside the weapon, he fled on along the corridor. He did not see a woman's dark face peer cautiously after him from behind a hanging. It vanished, and presenly Techotl groaned and stirred, rose dazedly and staggered drunkenly away, calling Conan's name.

Olmec hurried on down the corridor, and descended a winding ivory staircase. He crossed several corridors and halted at last in a broad chamber whose doors were veiled with heavy tapestries, with one exception—a heavy bronze door similar to the Door of the Eagle on the upper floor.

He was moved to rumble, pointing to it: "That is one of the outer doors of Tecuhltli. For the first time in fifty years it is unguarded. We need not guard it now, for Xotalanc is no more."

"Thanks to Conan and me, you bloody rogue!" sneered Valeria, trembling with fury and the shame of physical coercion. "You trecherous dog! Conan will cut your throat for this!"

Olmec did not bother to voice his belief that Conan's own gullet had already been severed according to his whispered command. He was too utterly cynical to be at all interested in her thoughts or opinions. His flame-lit eyes devoured her, dwelling burningly on the generous expanses of clear white flesh exposed where her shirt and breeches had been torn in the struggle.

"Forget Conan," he said thickly. "Olmec is lord of Xuchotl. Xotalanc is no more. There will be no more fighting. We shall spend our lives in drinking and love-making. First let us drink!"

He seated himself on an ivory table and pulled her down on his knees, like a dark-skinned satyr with a white nymph in his arms. Ignoring her un- nymphlike profanity, he held her helpless with one great arm about her waist while the other reached across the table and secured a vessel of wine.

"Drink!" he commanded, forcing it to her lips, as she writhed her head away.

The liquor slopped over, stinging her lips, splashing down on her naked breasts.

"Your guest does not like your wine, Olmec," spoke a cool, sardonic voice.

Olmec stiffened; fear grew in his flaming eyes. Slowly he swung his great head about and stared at Tascela who posed negligently in the curtained doorway, one hand on her smooth hip. Valeria twisted herself about in his iron grip, and when she met the burning eyes of Tascela, a chill tingled along her supple spine. New experiences were flooding Valeria's proud soul that night.

Recently she had learned to fear a man; now she knew what it was to fear a woman.

Olmec sat motionless, a gray pallor growing under his swarthy skin. Tascela brought her other hand from behind her and displayed a small gold vessel.

"I feared she would not like your wine, Olmec," purred the princess, "so I brought some of mine, some I brought with me long ago from the shores of Lake Zuad—do you understand, Olmec?"

Beads of sweat stood out suddenly on Olmec's brow. His muscles relaxed, and Valeria broke away and put the table between them. But though reason told her to dart from the room, some fascination she could not understand held her rigid, watching the scene.

Tascela came toward the seated prince with a swaying, undulating walk that was mockery in itself. Her voice was soft, slurringly caressing, but her eyes gleamed. Her slim fingers stroked his beard lightly.

"You are selfish, Olmec," she crooned, smiling. "You would keep our handsome guest to yourself, though you knew I wished to entertain her. You are much at fault, Olmec!"

The mask dropped for an instant; her eyes flashed, her face was contorted and with an appalling show of strength her hand locked convulsively in his beard and tore out a great handful. This evidence of unnatural strength was no more terrifying than the momentary baring of the hellish fury that raged under her bland exterior.

Olmec lurched up with a roar, and stood swaying like a bear, his mighty hands clenching and unclenching.

"Slut!" His booming voice filled the room. "Witch! She-devil! Tecuhltli should have slain you fifty years ago! Begone! I have endured too much from you! This white-skinned wench is mine! Get hence before I slay you!"

The princess laughed and dashed the blood-stained strands into his face. Her laughter was less merciful than the ring of flint on steel.

"Once you spoke otherwise, Olmec," she taunted. "Once, in your youth, you spoke words of love. Aye, you were my lover once, years ago, and because you loved me, you slept in my arms beneath the enchanted lotus—and thereby put into my hands the chains that enslaved you. You know you cannot withstand me. You know I have but to gaze into your eyes, with the mystic power a priest of Stygia taught me, long ago, and you are powerless. You remember the night beneath the black lotus that waved above us, stirred by no worldly breeze; you scent again the unearthly perfumes that stole and rose like a cloud about you to enslave you. You cannot fight against me. You are my slave as you were that night—as you shall be so long as you live, Olmec of Xuchotl!"

Her voice had sunk to a murmur like the rippling of a stream running through starlit darkness. She leaned close to the prince and spread her long tapering fingers upon his giant breast. His eyes glared, his great hands fell limply to his sides.

With a smile of cruel malice, Tascela lifted the vessel and placed it to his lips.

"Drink!"

Mechanically the prince obeyed. And instantly the glaze passed from his eyes and they were flooded with fury, comprehension and an awful fear. His mouth gaped, but no sound issued. For an instant he reeled on buckling knees, and then fell in a sodden heap on the floor.

His fall jolted Valeria out of her paralysis. She turned and sprang toward the door, but with a movement that would have shamed a leaping panther, Tascela was before her. Valeria struck at her with her clenched fist, and all the power of her supple body behind the blow. It would have stretched a man senseless on the floor. But with a lithe twist of her torso, Tascela avoided the blow and caught the pirate's wrist. The next instant Valeria's left hand was imprisoned and, holding her wrists together with one hand, Tasacela calmly bound them with a cord she drew from her girdle. Valeria thought she had tasted the ultimate in humiliation already that night, but her shame at being manhandled by Olmec was nothing to the sensations that now shook her supple frame. Valeria had always been inclined to despise the other members of her sex; and it was overwhelming to encounter another woman who could handle her like a child. She scarcely resisted at all when Tascela forced her into a chair and, drawing her bound wrists down between her knees, fastened them to the chair.

Casually stepping over Olmec, Tascela walked to the bronze door and shot the bolt and threw it open, revealing a hallway without.

"Opening upon this hall," she remarked, speaking to her feminine captive for the first time, "there is a chamber which in old times was used as a torture room. When we retired into Tecuhltli, we brought most of the apparatus with us, but there was one piece too heavy to move. It is still in working order. I think it will be quite convenient now."

An understanding flame of terror rose in Olmec's eyes. Tascela strode back to him, bent and gripped him by the hair.

"He is only paralyzed temporarily," she remarked conversationally. "He can hear, think, and feel—aye, he can feel very well indeed!"

With which sinister observation she started toward the door, dragging the giant bulk with an ease that made the pirate's eyes dilate. She passed into the hall and moved down it without hesitation, presently disappearing with her captive into a chamber that opened into it, and whence shortly thereafter issued the clank of iron.

Valeria swore softly and tugged vainly, with her legs braced against the chair. The cords that confined her were apparently unbreakable.

Tascela presently returned alone; behind her a muffled groaning issued from the chamber. She closed the door but did not bolt it. Tascela was beyond the grip of habit, as she was beyond the touch of other human instincts and emotions.

Valeria sat dumbly, watching the woman in whose slim hands, the pirate realized, her destiny now rested.

Tascela grasped her yellow locks and forced back her head, looking impersonally down into her face. But the glitter in her dark eyes was not impersonal.

"I have chosen you for a great honor," she said. "You shall restore the youth of Tascela. Oh, you stare at that! My appearance is that of youth, but through my veins creeps the sluggish chill of approaching age, as I have felt it a thousand times before. I am old, so old I do not remember my childhood. But I was a girl once, and a priest of Stygia loved me, and gave me the secret of immortality and youth everlasting. He died, then—some said by poison. But I dwelt in my palace by the shores of Lake Zuad and the passing years touched me not. So at last a king of Stygia desired me, and my people rebelled and brought me to this land. Olmec called me a princess. I am not of royal blood. I am greater than a princess. I am Tascela, whose youth your own glorious youth shall restore."

Valeria's tongue clove to the roof of her mouth. She sensed here a mystery darker than the degeneracy she had anticipated.

The taller woman unbound the Aquilonian's wrists and pulled her to her feet. It was not fear of the dominant strength that lurked in the princess' limbs that made Valeria a helpless, quivering captive in her hands. It was the burning, hypnotic, terrible eyes of Tascela.

7. — HE COMES FROM THE DARK

"Well, I'm a Kushite!"

Conan glared down at the man on the iron rack.

"What the devil are you doing on that thing?"

Incoherent sounds issued from behind the gag and Conan bent and tore it away, evoking a bellow of fear from the captive; for his action caused the iron ball to lurch down until it nearly touched the broad breast.

"Be careful, for Set's sake!" begged Olmec.

"What for?" demanded Conan. "Do you think I care what happens to you? I only wish I had time to stay here and watch that chunk of iron grind your guts out. But I'm in a hurry. Where's Valeria?"

"Loose me!" urged Olmec. "I will tell you all!"

"Tell me first."

"Never!" The prince's heavy jaws set stubbornly.

"All right." Conan seated himself on a near-by bench. "I'll find her myself, after you've been reduced to a jelly. I believe I can speed up that process by twisting my sword-point around in your ear," he added, extending the weapon experimentally.

"Wait!" Words came in a rush from the captive's ashy lips. "Tascela took her from me. I've never been anything but a puppet in Tascela's hands."

"Tascela?" snorted Conan, and spat. "Why, the filthy—"

"No, no!" panted Olmec. "It's worse than you think. Tascela is old – centuries old. She renews her life and her youth by the sacrifice of beautiful young women. That's one thing that has reduced the clan to its present state. She will draw the essence of Valeria's life into her own body, and bloom with fresh vigor and beauty."

"Are the doors locked?" asked Conan, thumbing his sword edge.

"Aye! But I know a way to get into Tecuhltli. Only Tascela and I know, and she thinks me helpless and you slain. Free me and I swear I will help you rescue Valeria. Without my help you cannot win into Tecuhltli; for even if you tortured me into revealing the secret, you couldn't work it. Let me go, and we will steal on Tascela and kill her before she can work magic—before she can fix her eyes on us. A knife thrown from behind will do the work. I should have killed her thus long ago, but I feared that without her to aid us the Xotalancas would overcome us. She needed my help, too; that's the only reason she let me live this long. Now neither needs the other, and one must die. I swear that when we have slain the witch, you and Valeria shall go free without harm. My people will obey me when Tascela is dead."

Conan stooped and cut the ropes that held the prince, and Olmec slid cautiously from under the great ball and rose, shaking his head like a bull and muttering imprecations as he fingered his lacerated scalp. Standing shoulder to shoulder the two men presented a formidable picture of primitive power. Olmec was as tall as Conan, and heavier; but there was something repellent about the Tlazitlan, something abysmal and monstrous that contrasted unfavorably with the clean-cut, compact hardness of the Cimmerian. Conan had discarded the remnants of his tattered, blood-soaked shirt, and stood with his remarkable muscular development impressively revealed. His great shoulders were as broad as those of Olmec, and more cleanly outlined, and his huge breast arched with a more impressive sweep to a hard waist that lacked the paunchy thickness of Olmec's midsection. He might have been an image of primal strength cut out of bronze. Olmec was darker, but not from the burning of the sun. If Conan was a figure out of the dawn of time, Olmec was a shambling, somber shape from the darkness of time's pre-dawn.

"Lead on," demanded Conan. "And keep ahead of me. I don't trust you any farther than I can throw a bull by the tail."

Olmec turned and stalked on ahead of him, one hand twitching slightly as it plucked at his matted beard.

Olmec did not lead Conan back to the bronze door, which the prince naturally supposed Tascela had locked, but to a certain chamber on the border of Tecuhltli.

"This secret has been guarded for half a century," he said. "Not even our own clan knew of it, and the Xotalancas never learned. Tecuhltli himself built this secret entrance, afterwards slaying the slaves who did the work for he feared that he might find himself locked out of his own kingdom some day because of the spite of Tascela, whose passion for him soon changed to hate. But she discovered the secret, and barred the hidden door against him one day as he fled back from an unsuccessful raid, and the Xotalancas took him and flayed him. But once, spying upon her, I saw her enter Tecuhltli by this route, and so learned the secret."

He pressed upon a gold ornament in the wall, and a panel swung inward, disclosing an ivory stair leading upward.

"This stair is built within the wall," said Olmec. "It leads up to a tower upon the roof, and thence other stairs wind down to the various chambers. Hasten!"

"After you, comrade!" retorted Conan satirically, swaying his broadsword as he spoke, and Olmec shrugged his shoulders and stepped onto the staircase. Conan instantly followed him, and the door shut behind them. Far above a cluster of fire-jewels made the staircase a well of dusky dragon-light.

They mounted until Conan estimated that they were above the level of the fourth floor, and then came out into a cylindrical tower, in the domed roof of which was set the bunch of fire-jewels that lighted the stair. Through gold-barred windows, set with unbreakable crystal panes, the first windows he had seen in Xuchotl, Conan got a glimpse of high ridges, domes and more towers, looming darkly against the stars. He was looking across the roofs of Xuchotl.

Olmec did not look through the windows. He hurried down one of the several stairs that wound down from the tower, and when they had descended a few feet, this stair changed into a narrow corridor that wound tortuously on for some distance. It ceased at a steep flight of steps leading downward. There Olmec paused.

Up from below, muffled, but unmistakable, welled a woman's scream, edged with fright, fury, and shame. And Conan recognized Valeria's voice.

In the swift rage roused by that cry, and the amazement of wondering what peril could wring such a shriek from Valeria's reckless lips, Conan forgot Olmec. He pushed past the prince and started down the stair. Awakening instinct brought him about again, just as Olmec struck with his great mallet-like fist. The blow, fierce and silent, was aimed at the base of Conan's brain. But the Cimmerian wheeled in time to receive the buffet on the side of his neck instead. The impact would have snapped the vertebrae of a lesser man. As it was, Conan swayed backward, but even as he reeled he dropped his sword, useless at such close quarters, and grasped Olmec's extended arm, dragging the prince with him as he fell. Headlong they went down the steps together, in a revolving whirl of limbs and heads and bodies. And as they went, Conan's iron fingers found and locked in Olmec's bull-throat.

The barbarian's neck and shoulder felt numb from the sledge-like impact of Olmec's huge fist, which had carried all the strength of the massive forearm, thick triceps and great shoulder. But this did not affect his ferocity to any appreciable extent. Like a bulldog he hung on grimly, rolled, until at last they struck an ivory panel-door at the bottom with such and impact, that they splintered its full length and crashed through its ruins. But Olmec was already dead, for those iron fingers had crushed out his life and broken his neck as they fell.

Conan rose, shaking the splinters from his great shoulders, blinking blood and dust out of his eyes.

He was in the great throne room. There were fifteen people in that room besides himself. The first person he saw was Valeria. A curious black altar stood before the throne-dais. Ranged about it, seven black candles in golden candlesticks sent up oozing spirals of thick green smoke, disturbingly scented. These spirals united in a cloud near the ceiling, forming a smoky arch above the altar. On that altar lay Valeria, stark naked, her white flesh gleaming in shocking contrast to the glistening ebon stone. She was not bound. She lay at full length, her arms stretched out above her head to their fullest extent. At the head of the altar knelt a young man, holding her wrists firmly. A young woman knelt at the other end of the altar, grasping her ankles. Between them she could neither rise nor move.

Eleven men and women of Tecuhltli knelt dumbly in a semicircle, watching the scene with hot, lustful eyes.

On the ivory throne-seat Tascela lolled. Bronze bowls of incense rolled their spirals about her; the wisps of smoke curled about her naked limbs like caressing fingers. She could not sit still; she squirmed and shifted about with sensuous abandon, as if finding pleasure in the contact of the smooth ivory with her sleek flesh.

The crash of the door as it broke beneath the impact of the hurtling bodies caused no change in the scene. The kneeling men and women merely glanced incuriously at the corpse of their prince and at the man who rose from the ruins of the door, then swung their eyes greedily back to the writhing white shape on the black altar. Tascela looked insolently at him, and sprawled back on her seat, laughing mockingly.

"Slut!" Conan saw red. His hands clenched into iron hammers as he started for her. With his first step something clanged loudly and steel bit savagely into his leg. He stumbled and almost fell, checked in his headlong stride. The jaws of an iron trap had closed on his leg, with teeth that sank deep and held. Only the ridged muscles of his calf saved the bone from being splintered. The accursed thing had sprung out of the smoldering floor without warning. He saw the slots now, in the floor where the jaws had lain, perfectly camouflaged.

"Fool!" laughed Tascela. "Did you think I would not guard against your possible return? Every door in this chamber is guarded by such traps. Stand there and watch now, while I fulfill the destiny of your handsome friend! Then I will decide your own."

Conan's hand instinctively sought his belt, only to encounter an empty scabbard. His sword was on the stair behind him. His poniard was lying back in the forest, where the dragon had torn it from his jaw. The steel teeth in his leg were like burning coals, but the pain was not as savage as the fury that seethed in his soul. He was trapped, like a wolf. If he had had his sword he would have hewn off his leg and crawled across the floor to slay Tascela. Valeria's eyes rolled toward him with mute appeal, and his own helplessness sent red waves of madness surging through his brain.

Dropping on the knee of his free leg, he strove to get his fingers between the jaws of the trap, to tear them apart by sheer strength. Blood started from beneath his fingernails, but the jaws fitted close about his leg in a circle whose segments jointed perfectly, contracted until there was no space between his mangled flesh and the fanged iron. The site of Valeria's naked body added flame to the fire of his rage.

Tascela ignored him. Rising languidly from her seat she swept the ranks of her subjects with a searching glance, and asked: "Where are Xamec, Zlanath and Tachic?"

"They did not return from the catacombs, princess," answered a man. "Like the rest of us, they bore bodies of the slain into the crypts, but they have not returned. Perhaps the ghost of Tolkemec took them."

"Be silent, fool!" she ordered harshly. "The ghost is a myth."

She came down from her dais, playing with a thin gold-hilted dagger. Her eyes burned like nothing on the hither side of hell. She paused beside the altar and spoke in the tense stillness.

"Your life shall make me young, white woman!" she said. "I shall lean upon your bosom and place my lips over yours, and slowly— ah, slowly! – sink this blade through your heart, so that your life, fleeing your stiffening body, shall enter mine, making me bloom again with youth and with life everlasting!"

Slowly, like a serpent arching toward its victim, she bent down through the writhing smoke, closer and closer over the now motionless woman who stared up into her glowing dark eyes— eyes that grew larger and deeper, blazing like black moons in the swirling smoke.

The kneeling people gripped their hands and held their breath, tense for the bloody climax, and the only sound was Conan's fierce panting as he strove to tear his leg from the trap.

All eyes were glued on the altar and the white figure there; the crash of a thunderbolt could hardly have broken the spell, yet it was only a low cry that shattered the fixity of the scene and brought all whirling about—a low cry, yet one to make the hair stand up stiffly on the scalp. They looked, and they saw.

Framed in the door to the left of the dais stood a nightmare figure. It was a man, with a tangle of white hair and a matted white beard that fell over his breast. Rags only partly covered his gaunt frame, revealing half-naked limbs strangely unnatural in appearance. The skin was not like that of a normal human. There was a suggestion of scaliness about it, as if the owner had dwelt long under conditions almost antithetical to those conditions under which human life ordinarily thrives. And there was nothing at all human about the eyes that blazed from the tangle of white hair. They were great gleaming disks that started unwinkingly, luminous, whitish, and without a hint of normal emotion or sanity. The mouth gaped, but no coherent words issued—only a high-pitched tittering.

"Tolkemec!" whispered Tascela, livid, while the others crouched in speechless horror. "No myth, then, no ghost! Set! You have dwelt for twelve years in darkness! Twelve years among the bones of the dead! What grisly food did you find? What mad travesty of life did you live, in the stark blackness of that eternal night? I see now why Xamec and Zlanath and Tachic did not return from the catacombs—and never will return. But why have you waited so long to strike? Were you seeking something, in the pits? Some secret weapon you knew was hidden there? And have you found it at last?"

That hideous tittering was Tolkemec's only reply, as he bounded into the room with a long leap that carried him over the secret trap before the door — by chance, or by some faint recollection of the ways of Xuchotl. He was not mad, as a man is mad. He had dwelt apart from humanity so long that he was no longer human. Only an unbroken thread of memory embodied in hate and the urge for vengeance had connected him with the humanity from which he had been cut off, and held him lurking near the people he hated. Only that thin string had kept him from racing and prancing off for ever into the black corridors and realms of the subterranean world he had discovered, long ago.

"You sought something hidden!" whispered Tascela, cringing back. "And you have found it! You remember the feud! After all these years of blackness, you remember!"

For in the lean hand of Tolkemec now waved a curious jade-hued wand, on the end of which glowed a knob of crimson shaped like a pomegranate. She sprang aside as he thrust it out like a spear, and a beam of crimson fire lanced from the pomegranate. It missed Tascela, but the woman holding Valeria's ankles was in the way. It smote between her shoulders. There was a sharp crackling sound and the ray of fire flashed from her bosom and struck the black altar, with a snapping of blue sparks. The woman toppled sidewise, shriveling and withering like a mummy even as she fell.

Valeria rolled from the altar on the other side, and started for the opposite wall on all fours. For hell had burst loose in the throne room of dead Olmec.

The man who had held Valeria's hands was the next to die. He turned to run, but before he had taken half a dozen steps, Tolkemec, with an agility appalling in such a frame, bounded around to a position that placed the man between him and the altar. Again the red fire-beam flashed and the Tecuhltli rolled lifeless to the floor, as the beam completed its course with a burst of blue sparks against the altar.

Then began the slaughter. Screaming insanely the people rushed about the chamber, caroming from one another, stumbling and falling. And among them Tolkemec capered and pranced, dealing death. They could not escape by the doors; for apparently the metal of the portals served like the metal veined stone altar to complete the circuit for whatever hellish power flashed like thunderbolts from the witch-wand the ancient waved in his hand. When he caught a man or a woman between him and a door or the altar, that one died instantly. He chose no special victim. He took them as they came, with his rags flapping about his wildly gyrating limbs, and the gusty echoes of his tittering sweeping the room above the screams. And bodies fell like falling leaves about the altar and at the doors. One warrior in desperation rushed at him, lifting a dagger, only to fall before he could strike. But the rest were like crazed cattle, with no thought for resistance, and no chance of escape.

The last Tecuhltli except Tascela had fallen when the princess reached the Cimmerian and the girl who had taken refuge beside him. Tascela bent and touched the floor, pressing a design upon it. Instantly the iron jaws released the bleeding limb and sank back into the floor.

"Slay him if you can!" she panted, and pressed a heavy knife into his hand. "I have no magic to withstand him!"

With a grunt he sprang before the woman, not heeding his lacerated leg in the heat of the fighting lust. Tolkemec was coming toward him, his weird eyes ablaze, but he hesitated at the gleam of the knife in Conan's hand. Then began a grim game, as Tolkemec sought to circle about Conan and get the barbarian between him and the altar or a metal door, while Conan sought to avoid this and drive home his knife. The women watched tensely, holding their breath.

There was no sound except the rustle and scrape of quick-shifting feet. Tolkemec pranced and capered no more. He realized that grimmer game confronted him than the people who had died screaming and fleeing. In the elemental blaze of the barbarian's eyes he read an intent deadly as his own. Back and forth they weaved, and when one moved the other moved as if invisible threads bound them together. But all the time Conan was getting closer and closer to his enemy. Already the coiled muscles of his thighs were beginning to flex for a spring, when Valeria cried out. For a fleeting instant a bronze door was in line with Conan's moving body. The red line leaped, searing Conan's flank as he twisted aside, and even as he shifted he hurled the knife. Old Tolkemec went down, truly slain at last, the hilt vibrating on his breast.

Tascela sprang—not toward Conan, but toward the wand where it shimmered like a live thing on the floor. But as she leaped, so did Valeria, with a dagger snatched from a dead man; and the blade, driven with all the power of the pirate's muscles, impaled the princess of Tecuhltli so that the point stood out between her breasts. Tascela screamed once and fell dead, and Valeria spurned the body with her heel as it fell.

"I had to do that much, for my own self-respect!" panted Valeria, facing Conan across the limp corpse.

"Well, this cleans up the feud," he grunted. "It's been a hell of a night! Where did these people keep their food? I'm hungry."

"You need a bandage on that leg." Valeria ripped a length of silk from a hanging and knotted it about her waist, then tore off some smaller strips which she bound efficiently about the barbarian's lacerated limb.

"I can walk on it," he assured her. "Let's begone. It's dawn, outside this infernal city. I've had enough of Xuchotl. It's well the breed exterminated itself. I don't want any of their accursed jewels. They might be haunted."

"There is enough clean loot in the world for you and me," she said, straightening to stand tall and splendid before him.

The old blaze came back in his eyes, and this time she did not resist as he caught her fiercely in his arms.

"It's a long way to the coast," she said presently, withdrawing her lips from his.

"What matter?" he laughed. "There's nothing we can't conquer. We'll have our feet on a ship's deck before the Stygians open their ports for the trading season. And then we'll show the world what plundering means!"

THE END